Lynne Bryan

GORGEOUS

SCEPTRE

First published in 1999 by Hodder and Stoughton
A division of Hodder Headline PLC
A Sceptre Book

10 9 8 7 6 5 4 3 2 1

A CIP catalogue record for this title is available from the British Library

ISBN 0 340 73968 1

Typeset by
Palimpsest Book Production Limited, Polmont, Stirlingshire
Printed and bound in Great Britain by
Mackays of Chatham PLC

Hodder and Stoughton
A division of Hodder Headline PLC
338 Euston Road
London NW1 3BH

\$ 9.95
A4
01 F

Gorgeous

A

Envy at the Cheese Handout

To Andrew and Rose

Acknowledgments

With thanks to my agent Jane Bradish-Ellames and my editor Carole Welch for their advice and support, to Eastern Arts for the grant, to Jenny Bryan for the housesitting info, to Rose for being Rose, and especially to Andrew Cowan for everything.

1

Morning

Rita turns into Ashberry Grove. She is still in fourth and her speeding car takes the corner wide. She travels some distance down the wrong side of the street.

Her passenger, Doreen, clasps her handbag tight, pushing it into her lap. Rita swerves to the left and Doreen inhales. Audibly. Uuhf. The sound is scared and Rita smiles.

Rita is after Doreen. She's paying her back. Because Doreen woke Rita early this morning. She phoned and her call dragged Rita from the juiciest dream, where she was in her office, as usual, in the violet twilight, licking the balls of a well-hung man.

Six forty-five a.m. A cheated Rita lay in bed, her mouth tasting metallic, her tongue furry, her eyes glued with sleep, the mobile cupped to her wax-blocked ear. 'Christ, Doreen,' she said, keeping her voice low to avoid disturbing her husband, Collis. 'This is short notice and it's a bad day for me. I've got a lot on.'

'I know. I know.' Doreen bleated. 'I know. I'm so

stupid. She wouldn't start last night but I didn't think it would be a problem. Mini Mouse has never let me down before. I've had her for years and she's been so brave and loyal. She's failed her MOT once, that's all.'

'You're talking about a piece of machinery, Doreen.'

'Mmm.'

'Machinery can't be relied on.'

Rita wonders why she didn't tell Doreen to catch the Early-Birds' Bus or call a cab. She wonders why she gave in so easily, relinquishing the pleasures of her fantasy fling. She attacks the gears, making them grate. A screech jangles the vehicle and she bellows over it, 'Number forty-seven?'

Doreen manages a squeak.

'The pink bungalow?' Rita peers through the windscreen. Lamp-posts, hedges, whiz by and her possible destination is coming up fast. Too fast. 'This pink bungalow?'

Doreen nods her head.

'Doreen answer!'

'Yeee—' she squeaks.

'Shit!' Rita slams on the brakes, and Doreen crashes into the dash, thwacking the glove-compartment door. It springs open. A mess of tissues, make-up, Filofax leaves, HRT patches, super-sized tampons, business papers and false fingernails spills to the floor.

'Bugger.' Rita switches off the engine, silently counts to ten, then turns to her employee. Doreen is crouched with her arms wrapped round her stomach, hugging herself. 'Sit back,' Rita orders, her heart skipping fast.

Doreen obliges. She raises herself and blinks blankly at Rita. Doreen is not the prettiest person but she has never looked frightful. She has never looked like this before. Her hair stands away from her scalp as if it has been shot through with electricity. A lump is showing on her brow, and there is a long graze across the bridge of her nose. Rita watches her carefully. She could be in trouble here.

'Are you okay?' Rita has to play this right.

'I think so.'

'Nothing going off inside? No pains?'

'Oh no.'

Rita turns the rear-view mirror towards Doreen. 'You have a small cut.'

Doreen stares at herself. 'Oh.' She puts a finger to her injury and smears the squirt of blood, pushing it about until it appears like someone has stamped a red question mark on her forehead.

Rita smiles sympathetically, but she does not say *sorry*: she has been in business long enough to know that apologies can cost. She briskly twists the mirror from Doreen and points at the Kleenex by the woman's sandalled feet. 'What you need is a tissue. Try one of those.'

Doreen sniffs. 'Thank you.' She collects a peach three-ply. She wipes it under her nose and under her eyes, but, for some reason, does not dab her cut. 'Thank you,' she says again. She puts the hanky in her dress pocket, then begins to feed Rita's spilled belongings back into the dash.

Rita relaxes; Doreen would sooner be hung and quartered than cause a scene. 'Don't worry about the mess,' says Rita. 'We must get on.'

Rita walks up the crazy-paved path to the pink bungalow. She walks quickly, tap-tapping along in her spiky high-heels, and Doreen trails after.

Doreen is loaded with luggage: a suitcase and handbag and three plastic carriers crammed with groceries. She huffs and puffs and Rita ignores her. It is nearly eight-fifteen and Rita wants to get shifting, to get to her office. She has a party to organise and, besides, she has helped Doreen enough. A lift! Would Rita have agreed to give any of her other sitters a lift? Sometimes Rita suspects Doreen of craftiness, playing weak to get her own way.

Rita reaches the front porch. 'What a stupid place to put a keyhole,' she grumbles. She bends low from the waist to examine it, and her large firm buttocks expand with the movement. She pokes a finger at the lock and asks tetchily, 'Are these people dwarves?'

'Oh no.' Doreen comes up behind, her breath escaping in whispery gasps. 'You've met them. Remember? Mr Gallagher is six foot something. He's a big man.'

'With a pea-brain.' Rita straightens. 'There's plenty of them about. Now, come on.' Rita regally holds out her hand.

'Pardon?' Doreen replies.

'Bungalow keys.'

'Oh yes.' Doreen ditches her luggage and hunts frantically. One of her carriers topples. It spills packets of frozen vegetables and ice-pops on her toes.

'Ooohhh!' Doreen kicks and twirls, and Rita watches the ballerina act and sighs. Doreen is an excellent housesitter – clients adore her deference, her conscientiousness – but she is so irritating, her flaps and panics are so very trying.

Doreen finds the keys in her dress pocket, and Rita wrests them from her jittery grasp. 'Thank you!' Then she bends from the waist again and her chunky buttocks and matching resolute legs root her steadfast to the ground as she works the mortice. The morning stirs around her.

'Alleluia!' Rita pushes her mannish palms down the sides of her skirt. She tugs the handle and opens the door to step into the tiny square porch. 'Terrible.' She raps its glass walls with her thick knuckles. 'Terrible. These frost up in the winter, boil in the summer. They're a haven for condensation and flies. Pass your bags, Doreen.'

Doreen lifts a carrier. She gives it to Rita. Rita gathers it to her chest, eyes its contents and smiles. 'You'll get fat,' she tells her employee, pointing to a clutch of chocolate bars.

Doreen blushes.

'Fat like me.' Rita pats her bum and Doreen appears worried. 'A joke,' Rita says.

Doreen looks down at the bilberry ice-pops which still lie scattered on the path. 'I'm not very good at jokes,' she frowns.

'Then you should loosen up,' advises Rita.

Doreen raises her head and her puppyish eyes give Rita the shivers.

'So.' Rita changes the subject. 'You'll be here a week? The Gallaghers return next Monday?'

Doreen nods.

Rita grabs the handle of Doreen's suitcase and pulls it into the porch. 'Jolly good,' she says as she lumps the case by a garden gnome, a shiny plastic version holding a rod and line, lying on its back, fishing the porch's unsavoury air. 'Be professional and ring me if there's any problem.'

Doreen nods again.

'And remember it's the do today at five. You can come for a couple of hours but lock up this place carefully and wear a nice dress and put some lipstick on. It should be fun but you'll have to make your own way over. I can't ferry you.'

The sun glints through the soft cloud which loosely hangs in the sky. It highlights the question mark on Doreen's forehead. 'I could get a taxi?' she ventures.

Rita smiles tightly. 'Now, there's a good idea.'

6

Another Morning

Rita spat on her mascara block. She took a tiny brush and rubbed it through the spit. She rubbed it backwards and forwards until the tablet beneath bubbled and melted to a thick black paste. She looked at herself in the bathroom mirror and, with a finger, stretched the skin at the corner of her eye. She then ran the brush over her lashes. She expertly twisted and twirled the brush to spread out the cosmetic evenly. She used its pointed tip to lift off a few unsightly blobs. She repeated the process on the other eye.

'Have you nearly done in there?' shouted Agnes, Rita's mother. She knocked on the bathroom door, a rapid rat-ta-tat.

'Mmm.' Rita took a pin from the side-pocket of her make-up bag. She poked its sharp end at a couple of lashes which had stuck together and deftly separated them.

'Only I'm going to have to do something about that damp,' Agnes persisted.

'You're always at that damp.' Rita blinked. 'I don't

know why you bother.' Two black smudges appeared on the soft pouches of skin under her eyes. She dabbed them away with toilet paper. 'Ready!'

'About time.' Agnes pushed open the door. 'You'll be late for work.'

'Bloody hell!' Rita backed against the wall. She pulled a face at the metal pail which stood by her mother's feet. It was full of steamy water and disinfectant. 'What a stink!'

'Don't be silly, Rita.' Agnes grabbed the pail's handle and swung it into the chilly room and Rita raised her arms.

'No, no, get it away from me!'

Agnes didn't smile. 'Sometimes...' She stopped. Slowly she looked Rita up and down, eyeing the black fishnets, mini-skirt and skinny-rib top.

'Don't,' Rita warned. 'I can dress how I like.'

'Oh, Rita.'

'Oh, nothing. I am twenty years old.'

Agnes took a pair of rubber gloves from her housecoat pocket and tugged them on. 'But there's no need,' she said. 'Not for work.' The gloves were a jaunty orange but the rest of Agnes was grey. Her skin and lips were pale grey and her hair dark grey. Her housecoat was dark grey too. It had been navy but Agnes had squeezed the dye from it by repeatedly putting it through the mangle after its many washes. It was dark grey and it hung limply.

'I like dressing up. Dressing up makes me feel good.' Rita nodded at her mother's housecoat. 'You should try.'

Agnes dropped to her knees. She put a hand in the pail, bringing out a sparsely tufted scrubbing brush. 'Just leave me be, Rita.'

Rita looked at the clock above the mantelpiece in the

living room and set her watch by it. It was eight-forty. She had twenty minutes to get to work. There was no rush.

Rita lived with her parents in a two-up two-down (or three-down, if you counted the bathroom extension, which her mother did). When she'd been younger and smaller the house had seemed spacious, particularly because she was an only child and had a bedroom to herself. Most of her friends in the street had to share their sleeping space with their brothers and sisters and the family pets, and in comparison Rita's room with its single divan and lone dressing-table and chair had seemed enormous.

But now Rita's bedroom sat tightly round her. It cramped her. Like the whole house cramped her. Rita only had to take four big steps to cross from one side of the living room to the other. The kitchen was little more than a corridor – turn one way and you were face to face with the sink, turn the other and you were confronting the cooker. And Rita couldn't move without touching the fabric of the building – the walls were streaked with rub marks from her and her parents' shoulders – and she couldn't move without bumping into furniture or her mother and father.

Her mother was the greatest obstacle. On an endless cycle of cleaning, she wouldn't, couldn't stop, and Rita was constantly falling over buckets of water, dishcloths, bottles of disinfectant, mops, feather dusters and her mother's hunched body. Her mother knelt on a rubber mat for the floors and low corners. The mat was shaped like a kidney. It was perished round the edges and it had two smooth patches worn into it by her knees. Those patches knotted Rita's heart.

Rita took down her work-overall and jacket from the coat-pegs in the hall. She dropped the jacket at the foot of the stairs and bundled the pink nylon overall into her bag. The overall was uncomfortable and unflattering. The material was slippery and full of static and trapped Rita's body-heat so that by the end of the working day she was cooked. It had large ugly buttons and, worse, a humiliating embroidered pocket positioned square on the left breast which read *McGee's Fancy Underwear.*

Rita put on her jacket and zipped it up. She looped her bag over her shoulder and left the house. 'Bye,' she shouted to her mother as she shut the front door behind her. She caught no reply.

Rita lived in Cranley City, in a working-class neighbourhood called Crossforth Devices. The Devices was a network of narrow streets and alleys and terraced houses bordering the Crossforthian Stretch, a length of canal that joined The Midlands to The North. The canal used to be thick with the toing and froing of transportation barges, and the Devices had been home to the barge and warehouse workers and their families. But not any more. Now the canal was idle and the terraced houses were owned by the District Council, who rented them out to Cranley's needy.

The area's predominant colour was the colour of the paving slabs, the roof slates, the roads. A sludgy grey which mirrored the stagnant canal and reminded Rita of her mother's housecoat and of heavy stormy skies. There were a few whitewashed doorsteps and the Council had painted the window-frames and doors of the houses a sunny yellow. But these dabs of brightness jarred. They seemed to be trying too hard.

Rita crossed her street and headed for the alley which led to McGee's Fancy Underwear. She peered into the yards of the houses as she strolled along. They were functional spaces with no daisy-dotted lawns, though occasionally you might spy a shrub, a rose-bush pruned to a stump. They were home to prams and washing lines and dustbins, and each one nursed an extension, a chamber tacked on to the house's rear, a single-storey flat-roofed oblong.

The extensions had been built ten years before as part of the Council's drive to improve living conditions. Rita could remember how exciting it had been to receive the news: they were going to get an indoor loo and a proper bath! There was going to be an end to the indignities and humiliations she'd suffered. Such as:

The tin tub.

Agnes used to drag this monster in from the yard every Friday. She squeezed it into the kitchen and then filled it with pails of geyser-heated water.

Rita's father, Ernest, took his turn to clean himself and Agnes took hers and then Rita was ordered in. The water would have a crust on it by this time. Invariably. A plate of lathered soap and dirt scarred with nails (Ernest used to cut his toe-nails in the tub) and threaded with pubic hair. It was disgusting, and it visibly demonstrated to Rita her true position in the family. Third-in-line. Down among the detritus.

The strip-wash.

Agnes used to strip Rita and stand her in the sink for a clean on non-bath nights. At first Rita had been too young to be aware of the man next-door. But gradually, uncomfortably, she began to sense his eyes on her through the uncurtained kitchen window. Agnes seemed oblivious, lost in her rhythmical buffing and polishing of Rita's fresh skin. Rita tried to tell her, pointing to the man as he peered over the fence, and occasionally Agnes would look across. But the sly old bugger pretended to be busy then, putting rubbish in his bin, and Agnes would snap, 'He's just doing what he has to do, Rita. It's a free world.'

The karzy.

Rita never liked it: the freezing dark and flimsy lean-to at the end of the yard. It shook in the wind and had a dodgy latch. Often the latch would spring undone and the door would flap open to reveal Ernest scooping his penis back into his pants or Agnes sitting vulnerable, her sensible beige drawers inelegantly hooped round her ankles.

Rita left the alley and turned the corner for McGee's. Ahead, at the far end of the road, were two large cranes, their necks and arms reaching high into the dour Crossforthian sky. Thick cables trailed from the arms into the building site below. The site was surrounded by a loose-knitted metal fence, and Rita could see the materials stacked behind: the mounds of bricks and concrete tubing yet to be used, the wigwams of scaffolding waiting to be erected. She could see the men already at work and she could hear them whistling and shouting, tiny sounds almost swamped by the brumming lorries and the rhythmical churning of the mixers. Rita knew what was being built on the site. Every Crossforthian knew. Rita just didn't feel as good about it as most.

It had taken only two winters for their bathroom extension to lose its shine: for the flat roof to develop cracks, for water to drip from the window and walls, for a speckly damp to flourish. The Council's maintenance team had responded by installing a heater and an extractor fan and another air-vent. But the room's condition hadn't improved. Then the Council's housing department had sent an apologetic circular to Rita's parents explaining what was wrong and who was to blame and how they were not alone (all the extensions were affected, none had escaped) and why it might be more viable in the long-term to demolish the terraces and transfer the tenants to purpose-built high-rises of modern, storage-heated, double-glazed, superbly-plumbed flats. The project had been scheduled for 1964. It was now 1967 and the work had only just begun.

There was a sign fixed to the gates which opened into the site. Rita couldn't read it from where she was standing but she knew it by heart. It was reproduced in the *Cranley Gazette* often enough: the words HOMES FOR A NEW AGE, and the bold graphic of two slim towers pitched by the canal. Rita's parents would point it out to her, looking forward to the day when the flats would be finished and they could move in. They had high hopes.

Unlike Rita, who couldn't be persuaded by the talk of regeneration, by the jaunty feel that the bright orange diggers and dump-trucks had brought to the Devices. Because she was convinced that nothing now could change what was endemic in Crossforth's earth and sky and air. The bleakness and disappointment. There was too much of it to set right.

13

Morning Still

'Hello Gorgeous!'

'Morning Decrepit.' Rita slams shut her car door, places her handbag, cosmetics case and mound of papers on the vehicle's roof. She waits for Bill, the owner of Take Five Video Store, to sidle across and pat her bum. Their greetings have evolved over the years into this familiar exchange. Rita loves it. She smiles as Bill's thick fingers press against her buttocks. She enjoys being touched by this man.

She turns to face him. 'How are you?' He is tall, gangster-muscley with hefty thighs. His skin has a leathery texture. His eyes are small, set deep, and are shaded by a pair of vital brows. Rita has had sex with him, a bout of fast sex in the stockroom at the rear of his video store. She has never regretted it, never felt the urge to confess it to her husband, Collis, but neither has she repeated it. She tells herself she is too busy for a lengthy dalliance, for complications. She tells herself this often. 'Ready for work?'

'Ready for squashing Josie,' Bill replies. He watches

Rita as she locks her car door. Gold bracelets drop from beneath her jacket sleeve to jingle around her wrist. The noise is carefree, chiming with the summeriness of the day, the yellowy light which dances across the shop owners' car park.

'Has she bust the computer again?' asks Rita, gathering up her belongings.

'She reckons the Hoover did it. She plugged it in and hey presto! My hard disc is buggered and all I'm left with is a useless floppy.'

'Shame,' Rita says. 'A limp one.'

'Yes,' Bill replies. 'But that's not the point. She's a liability.'

'Ah, poor Bill.'

Rita chucks him under the chin, then heads for the back entrance to her agency – a wooden door, stained green and topped with a silver awning. Bill follows her.

'Keys in your pocket?' he asks.

Rita nods, and feels a happy tingle as Bill runs a hand over her skirt. 'I could get a long lunch-break,' he suggests, using a digit to caress the rounded mound of her stomach, then to hook the large bunch of office keys from their resting place.

'Impossible,' Rita replies. She looks up at him. 'It'll be a madhouse today. Remember?'

Bill takes Rita's hand and opens it. He lays the keys on her palm. 'Yes. Of course.' His square fingertips brush her false and brightly painted nails. 'But there's no harm in trying, is there?' He smiles.

'No.' Rita smiles too. 'There's no harm in that.'

Rita takes off her jacket, hangs it on the coat-rack outside the staff toilet. She squirts a jet of cleaner around the spotless toilet bowl, then rolls down her pants and squats. She watches herself in the mirror opposite. She is one helluva woman. She is forty-eight years old, she is going through the Change and is on medication, but she is not diminished. Sometimes she feels like her skin can hardly contain her, her energy, her ideas, her ambition. She feels fit to burst.

She wipes herself, pulls her pants up over the lacy threads of her suspender belt. She flushes the toilet, and leaves her reflection with a wink. She puts on the kettle to boil. Then she pulls back the louvre partition which separates the staff amenities and storeroom from her agency proper.

Rita's Housesitting Service is situated in Elysium, an area in Cranley favoured by Rita because there's no canal and there are no high-rises, no dole offices, no factories or council buildings, because it's like chalk to the Devices' cheese.

The agency is sandwiched between the Take Five Video Store and Garsten Street's Delicatessen and Restaurant. It used to be a newsagent's, and when Rita bought and converted it she retained its front window, a huge display-pane which the newsagent had plastered with advertisements, special offer notices, postcards tendering household items and dubious services. Collis suggested she board up the window to make her agency appear discreet, like a solicitor's or an accountant's. But Rita wanted to be open and visible to passers-by. She wanted shoppers to look through the window, to be drawn into her business because they could see it, see how clean and efficient and stylish her work-place was, how attractive and personable the staff.

Rita's sons helped her to do out the storeroom and staff quarters and Collis supervised, but Rita wouldn't let them touch the front office-space. She had her friend Celia design it, then she brought in professional decorators to fulfil Celia's vision.

Rita's decision was wise. Celia isn't trained but she's

always wrapped birthday and Christmas presents beautifully and she subscribes to *Domicile* and its bi-monthly supplement *Creative Home Decor.* Celia took to the job enthusiastically, choosing to wear paint-splattered dungarees and a pencil behind her ear, deciding on an earthy theme, a solid unfussy feel which would reassure customers. And so the agency walls are covered with pine and trimmed with skirting stained bottle-green. The carpet is made from coconut husk which has been plaited and coiled. A luxurious, lime two-seater sofa sits at an angle to the display-window. A potted fern stands behind it, a low pine coffee-table in front. The filing cabinets, desks and chairs and the awnings above the exterior doors provide a contrast. They are silver and very shiny. 'Signatures of modernity,' explained Celia. 'You, Rita, are the welcoming forest, the Mother Earth, but you are not old-fashioned. You are brisk, you are wise to the advantages of technology, you are clued-up. A dependable yet with-it operation.'

Rita walks though the space to release the roller blind pulled down over the display window. *Rita's Housesitting Service* is stencilled in large silver letters on the blind. The letters form an enthusiastic arc as though some force has exploded beneath them, pushing them upwards to kiss the sky. The summer sun illuminates the agency's name and seeps through the loosely-woven fabric of the blind. Gentle, misty dots of light splash the carpet and walls.

Rita flips the blind – it disappears inside itself, furling tightly and compliantly – and she surveys the street outside. The pavements are scrubbed-looking and chalky-white, the road newly covered with a fresh layer of glossy black tar. There are large Victorian houses opposite, and beyond them and around them are smaller, newer semis built from a lovely cream brick. Every home has a car or two, and a security system – alarm boxes sit above front doors and occasionally break the cosy silence with their fretful whine.

It is five years to the day since Rita set up here and the party she's holding this tea-time is to celebrate. It's a slap on the back for her staying the course; more, for making her business a success. She has over one hundred of Elysium's residents on her books, and she also has clients from Greenacres (the poshest area in Cranley) and beyond. The agency's high-ranking postcode along with Rita's aptitude have proved a real draw. Rita's phones are hot. Her engagement diary is chock-a-block.

For example – Rita wipes a fleck of dirt from the agency window – she has an appointment this morning with a Mr Arnold, a company director whose business affairs take him abroad for three months in every twelve. He lives just across the road and wishes to discuss the possibility of entrusting his property to Rita while he is away.

He was insistent that the matter should be discussed on the tenth, and Rita couldn't put him off, and now she faces a day which is packed too tightly. Besides Mr Arnold, she has an interview with a job-seeker, and she has those regular office duties (opening the mail, answering calls) which *cannot* be shelved until after the party, and she must prepare for the do itself. It's going to be frantic, and she's promised her assistants, Philippa and Nolene, time and a half to keep them eager. But even so.

Rita looks at her watch. It's nearly nine. Philippa will be late because she's collecting party decorations from the cash'n'carry on her way in, but Nolene is due any moment. Rita reverses the sign hanging on the glass-panelled agency door, CLOSED FOR NOW becoming WELCOME TO RITA'S HOUSESITTING SERVICE. WE ARE HERE TO HELP YOU, and as she does so she spies the number 30 at the bus-stop along the road.

The yellow double-decker trundles away and Rita sees Philippa (and only Philippa) heading towards the agency. Typical. Nolene time-keeps like a broken alarm clock, whereas Philippa is an Accurist set early. Rita waves at her more conscientious assistant, knowing for certain who she prefers.

Philippa is dressed for the agency do in a floaty blue two-piece. Her long hair is brushed and shiny. She has a wide tortoiseshell bangle on one arm, and tucked against her side is a large carton. She doesn't notice Rita's greeting. She walks self-consciously with her head bowed, and Rita smiles, realising why. On the front of the carton is a raunchy drawing of a man clutching a sausage-shaped balloon between his thighs. *Barry's Bangers and Party Playthings* is inscribed beneath. Philippa is embarrassed.

19

Philippa

I've been working for Mrs Rita Swales for over three years. Previously I was a dentist's assistant. That was a horrible job. I don't like medical things; the nitty-gritty of bodies; the pain. I started looking for an alternative position when the dentist, Mr Thompson, who wasn't particularly good at pulling teeth (he could fill but he couldn't extract), made a mess of a little girl's mouth. Her name was Gemma, she was only six, and I had to pad Gemma's gums with cotton swabs because the blood wouldn't stop. She was in tears and her mother was in tears and Mr Thompson was pretending all had gone to plan and there was nothing to worry about. He didn't apologise to Gemma and so I handed in my notice.

Mrs Swales doesn't apologise either. I need to get some agency stuff to the printer's soon and I'm having to nag Mrs Swales to check bits through. She's responded quite nastily and hasn't said sorry once. But then businesswomen have to dispense with their manners and harden up, get horrid, because it's a dog-eat-ladydog world out there. I am aware of this. I understand. Which is why I'm prepared to put up with Mrs Swales's sharp tongue.

Also, I love my job. I love what Rita's Housesitting Service has brought to my life. I'm dealing with the public but I'm not having to peer inside their orifices. And I've discovered I'm excellent at admin. I just have a feel for paper – for stapling paper, filing paper, folding paper. It's great. The office is bright and clean. The conditions are good. And I'm responsible for running the agency when Mrs Swales is on holiday. Also, I think the job has prospects because the agency has a brilliant reputation and seems to be on the up and up, and I know Mrs Swales is going to need a right-hand woman soon and I think she'll consider me because she hasn't the time to shop around, and she can't afford to take a leap in the dark either, to risk making a mistake, because she has a disabled husband and four kids to look out for.

Mrs Swales has a lot to shoulder. I don't envy her that but I do admire her. She is like one of those amazing women you see on telly chat shows who triumph over everything. She was born in Crossforth and she used to work in a knicker factory. She has no academic qualifications, no business degree. She has struggled for most of her life. But here she is! The owner and manageress of Rita's Housesitting Service. A success, a shining example to us all.

The Employee

McGee's Fancy Underwear stood next to Cranley's Industrial Laundry. The laundry was based in a red-bricked barn of a building, and McGee's inhabited a small outhouse tacked to its side.

Rita had gone to work at the laundry on leaving school. She'd been a sorter and had spent her nine-to-fives separating the incoming washing into three piles: whites, coloureds, repairs. She'd also had to empty garment pockets, rid them of items which might damage the cleaning equipment or ruin the finish. This had been a perk – by the end of each day Rita had often collected a tidy sum of lost ha'pennies, pennies, tanners and shillings – and initially it had made up for the boredom she'd felt, and the sickness. But after a few months she'd had enough. No amount of found treasure could compensate for the burning in her eyes (brought on by the acrid laundering fluids) or the tightness in her chest (caused by the dry steam puffing unceasingly from the presses). Rita had wanted out.

It had been easy for her to get another job. McGee's

had been looking for machinists and had put a notice on the board outside their reception. Rita had approached the woman behind the desk diffidently, hesitantly. 'Excuse me ... those jobs ... are you still taking people on? Like me ...? Would you take me on? I've no experience of sewing.'

'Good.' The thick-necked woman had smiled. 'No experience means no bad habits. Mr McGee prefers novices. We'll train you up. It only takes a week.' She handed Rita a form to complete, and afterwards measured her for a pink overall. 'You'll only get the one, so you'll have to wash it at weekends. They hold in the sweat,' she confided.

'So, you're giving me a job?' Rita had looked round the office. There were posters pinned to the grubby beige walls: posters of flowery bloomers, and bras made from shiny white fabric dotted with sequins. She'd felt excited; this had to be better than sifting through boiler suits and hospital pyjamas.

'You can start next Monday. Bring your National Insurance number. Then if you're good we'll give you 10 per cent discount on our best lines, 20 per cent on the less popular, and free seconds. You'll never have to worry about being run over by a bus ever again.'

'Celia!' Rita waved to her friend who was in the queue of women edging through the open factory gates. 'Wait for us.'

'Rita!' Celia stepped from the line. She looked classy, like a window-dressed mannequin. Her pink overall was hidden beneath a light green swing-coat. She wore pointy cream sling-backs and a cream headband. Her make-up was pale and sat smoothly on her lovely skin. She was Crossforth's elegant brunette; Rita was its brassy blonde.

A gang of boys opposite wolf-whistled and jeered.

They stood outside the iron railings which bordered Crossforth High: teenage boys in narrow-legged trousers and purple school blazers. Rita grimaced at them and Celia mouthed something, but they continued to fool around, ogling Rita and Celia, drawing womanly forms with their adolescent hands.

'Can't you lip read?' Rita shouted. 'The lady said "Bugger off!"'

'Oh Rita!' The middle-aged women pushing into McGee's tut-tutted but Rita wouldn't be checked, and her younger work colleagues encouraged her by clapping and giggling as she yelled at the gang some more.

'Ooer!' the boys responded, jiggling their loose gangly limbs. A monkeyish display which Rita and Celia saw most days through the window beside their work-bench.

McGee's Fancy Underwear consisted of three making-up rooms, one packing-and-distribution room, and sundry small offices. Rita and Celia were based in the making-up room which looked on to the street.

It was narrow and cramped, full of hefty oblong tables on which were screwed copper-coloured overlocking machines. The air was riddled with the whirr and buzz of the machines, the chatter of women (there were no male 'makers'), and the clank of trolleys which brought and collected the underwear. Bits of cotton thread and elastic and material scraps floated and fluttered moth-like around the room, and pale rays of light pushed through its barred and small-paned windows.

Rita and Celia had started at McGee's at the same time. The supervisor, Mrs Betsy Latham, whose hair was never out of rollers, had put them together on a double-bench. 'You're lucky,' Betsy had said, giving Rita the seat closest to the wall. She'd pointed to the square of speckled glass set into the unpainted masonry. 'You've got a view. You can see the boys and girls come out to play.'

But for a long time neither Rita nor Celia appreciated it. They were too busy: struggling to learn how to stitch quickly without puckering fabric and elastic, how to turn corners without getting fingers pierced by the sharp overlocking needles, how to begin a join and how to finish off; struggling to get used to each other, to bond.

Crossforth was small. Rita and Celia had been through its schools together and had frequented the same youth clubs and cafés but they'd skirted each other. Rita had considered Celia a snob, and Celia had felt intimidated by Rita's show. But now Rita and Celia were a team, and Rita regarded Celia as her closest friend.

Rita, though grateful to have escaped from the laundry, had soon become disappointed with McGee's. The work was mindless and repetitive; every day there were piles of panty-girdles, cotton-gussets and high-waisters to stitch. But Celia's sophisticated appearance, her film-starriness, provided a distraction. Also, she was a laugh. Celia was good at jokes and wasn't afraid (though she looked as if butter-wouldn't-melt) of talking rude, of being crude about Crossforth High's adolescent males.

The school could not contain its pupils. Every hour of the day there'd be kids loitering in the tarmacadamed grounds. They'd press themselves against the railings to intimidate passers-by; they'd huddle in groups to smoke cigarettes; they'd play tag round the five huge bins lined up outside the dining hall. They were quiet delinquents. Their actions were accompanied by a hush-hush, as if they believed silence would render them invisible, undetectable. Rita and Celia would watch the truants through their window and it would be like watching the telly with no sound. But it was a different experience at school break-times when these kids would be joined by a flood of others. Then – whah! – the noise would blast over the whirr of McGee's machines.

Rita and Celia preferred the breaks not because they were riotous but because there were more young men to stare at, to assess and rate. Rita and Celia graded the boys for looks, poise, confidence. They speculated on how the fanciable ones would grow; whether their handsomeness would improve or whether this was it, their beautiful moment. There were few stars. Most of them, even the pretty ones, were reduced, made ugly, by the testosterone which coursed through them. They were wankers, and Rita and Celia recognised this and would nudge-nudge and whisper, 'All dong, no brain.'

Recently though, Celia had lost interest in their game, preferring to moon about Fred, a crane-driver who worked on the twin towers' site by the canal. Fred was married with thinning hair. He came with plenty of baggage. But this made him appreciative of Celia's charms, keen (and able) to please her. 'Maturity,' Celia enthused. 'You can't beat it.' And Rita had felt no need to dispute this, until, that is, she spied a stranger in the yard.

Rita didn't know where he'd sprung from, whether the boy was a new arrival at the High or whether he'd been a weedy pre-pubertal type who'd suddenly put on muscley weight and height. Whatever. He stood apart. Even when surrounded by other pupils, his friends, admiring girls, he stood apart. He'd lean against the school's only tree. He'd press his head, his shoulders, his backside against its skinny trunk. He'd bend one long leg, flatten the sole of his shoe against the chipped and scored bark, and he'd look slowly, appraisingly about. Sometimes he would glance at the factories, and then Rita imagined he could see her through the small-paned window. He affected Rita. His eyes meeting her eyes.

She felt he was special, and, despite his youth, she wanted him.

Rita turned to enter the factory.

'Hang on a minute.' Celia grabbed Rita's arm. 'Do you see what I see? Near the High? Where has *he* come from?'

'Who?' Rita sucked in a breath and spun round, hoping it wouldn't be the boy, wanting to keep him a secret still, for herself alone.

'Gorgeous,' Celia swooned. It was him. 'Ripe.'

'Lay off,' snapped Rita, bolting suddenly across the road.

'Ooer!' said the monkey-legged yobs watching her pass. 'Ooer!'

'Hey!' Rita shouted to the boy. What was she doing?

'Hey!' he replied.

'Hey!' Rita persisted, calling out even as she reached him.

His tie was knotted loose and pulled away from the collar of a white crease-resistant shirt. The top button of the shirt was undone and there, displayed, was his thick body hair, curling from his chest to lace his beefy neck. He was smiling wide. 'Hey!' He had little white teeth and his gums were pale and prominent. His lips were dry but shapely, and Rita knew, now, what it was she was doing.

'I want to see you,' she said.

The Employer

'I've had a terrible journey, Mrs Swales,' Philippa says. 'The names I've been called.' She places the carton from Barry's Bangers and Party Playthings on her desk, and Rita looks at the graphic stamped on the carton's sides.

Rita smiles. The image might've been lifted from a lads' comic; one of those publications favoured by Rita's sons which luxuriate in bodily dysfunctions, depicting explosive farts, pus-filled boils, fleshy protuberances. Silly, harmless fun, Rita decides, and she asks, 'What kind of names, Philippa?'

'Unrepeatable, Mrs Swales. Really rude.' Philippa shakes her head. 'I feel like I've been stripped to my nothings on the number 30.'

Philippa wears her usual perfume. Rita can smell its sweetness, the gentle old-fashioned mix of lavender and rose. 'I'm sure it wasn't that bad,' she says. 'Take the box through to the back, and calm down. Make a pot of tea. The kettle's just boiled.'

Philippa crosses the office floor, her low-heeled sandals making flat, hollow noises as they meet with the matting. 'What makes people behave like that?' she complains. 'Is it the heat?'

'Philippa,' Rita replies, flicking through her keys, searching for the one which undoes the mail-box. 'Shush now.'

Rita finds the key, inserts it in the lock and gives it a twist. The box bottom springs open and a mound of letters falls out. There are the usual bills. Rita spots them immediately but she spies promising stuff also – red, grey and cream envelopes, A4 and A5 manilas, a scrappy-looking item with a recycled label Sellotaped around it, and an aerogramme. Rita crouches and gathers them tight to her chest, takes them to the lime two-seater sofa. The phone rings as she sits.

'Will you get it?' she shouts to her assistant, and Philippa – with a pint of milk in one hand – hurries in from the staff quarters.

'Rita's Housesitting Service, how may I help you?'

Rita spreads out the mail beside her. She selects a package and holds it to the light, shaking it, turning it this way and that. She feels excited. She slides a fingernail under its glued flap. She cannot help it. Opening the mail is Rita's treat. For her it makes every day, even the most unpromising, feel like Christmas.

'Oh Derek,' sighs Philippa. 'What is it this time?'

Dear me. Rita puts down the package. Derek is bad news. He is one of Rita's clumsier housesitters. He is adored by the clients because he is fastidious and a great cook and always leaves a little culinary something to welcome them home. Rita has received letters in praise of him – *What a lovely surprise. I returned from my holiday jet-lagged and shattered to find an immaculate house and a beautifully iced marble cake. Such a light sponge! Many congratulations to the chef!* – which is why Derek has never been given his cards. But his lubberliness is a liability. Two cups separated from their handles, a broken portable TV aerial, red wine spilt on an Irish linen tablecloth, a gashed stair banister and a clogged lavatory. These are his most recent calamities, and Rita watches Philippa's face, wanting to know, yet not wanting to know.

Philippa's jaw slackens. Her mouth goes into an O. 'Derek!' she almost squeals. 'On today of all days! How on earth—?'

Rita jumps from the sofa and grabs the phone. 'I'll take this.'

'But Mrs Swales—' Philippa objects.

'Yes. Yes.' Rita flaps a hand, shooing Philippa away. 'Now, Derek.' Rita turns her attention to the caller. 'Mrs Swales here, and skip the apologies. Is it major or minor?'

Derek hesitates, and Rita feels her neck muscles tensing. 'Minorish,' Derek finally concedes. 'Verging on the major—'

'Derek! *Spit it out!* '

Rita rings the Ripping Repairs subsidiary of Crazy Covers At Crazy Prices.

'What can we do for you, Mrs Swales?' asks the receptionist.

Rita describes how Derek has torn the covering on Mr Clayman's chaise-longue. The sitter tripped over Mr Clayman's indolent Siamese while carrying a plate of kebabs. The kebabs flew from the plate and some stained and two skewered the plump velveteen. ('We were so lucky,' Derek ventured. 'It could've been the cat, or my feet. I could have pierced toes!') 'It's urgent,' Rita says.

The receptionist consults a diary, Rita hears pages being turned. 'We can send a boy over next Tuesday,' the receptionist suggests.

'Too late.'

'We *are* heavily booked.'

‘Not good enough.’

‘You won’t get a better service elsewhere.’

‘I’m not going elsewhere. Put me through to Mr Richmond. Please.’

The receptionist grumpily transfers Rita to hold – ‘He’s a very busy man. I can’t guarantee he’ll be in his office’ – and Rita’s ear is blasted with *‘You’ve either got or you haven’t got style’*.

Stevie Richmond, the boss of Ripping Repairs and Crazy Covers At Crazy Prices and the clothes cash’n’-carry Dandy Duds, is in his fifties and wears a spangly suit which he swears *hasn’t* been made from a roll of his cheapest and shiniest upholstery fabric. He’s flash and employs lots of BIG women.

‘I enjoy patting bums,’ he drunkenly confessed to Rita at her New Year party. ‘Decent solid arses of the matronly-type.’ He winked at Rita and she fake-smiled and held on to her glass of red, willing herself not to chuck it at Richmond’s off-white cumberband. ‘*J’adore* broad broads!’ he continued.

The K-Tel compilation of Twenty Rag-Trade Faves ceases and Rita has Stevie Richmond coughing in her ear. ‘Stevie! Is that you, love?’

‘Rita, darling!’ Stevie is smoking a cigar. Rita hears him drawing on it. ‘Business or pleasure?’

‘Business.’

‘Shame.’

‘And pleasure.’

‘Aaah.’

Rita outlines her problem, then reminds Stevie Richmond about her do this afternoon. ‘Lots of booze and canapés. Captain Salcott will do a piece about it for the *Gazette*, but mainly it’s for fun. A glad-rags bash.’

‘And you’re wearing? Let me guess. Tassels?’

‘No, but slinky.’

‘Aaah, slinky?’

'Yes, very slinky. Slinky and short.'

'*Decolletée*?'

Rita grimaces. Stevie likes his French. '*Mais oui,*' she attempts. '*Decolletée.*'

'*Ooh la la! Très bon.*'

'So, you'll come then?'

'*Bien sur*,' Stevie smarms. 'You've persuaded me.'

'But before that?'

'Well, *ma cherie*, I shall send Dominic. This very afternoon. He's a whiz with the fluids and can do near-invisible mends.'

Rita smiles a wide smile. 'Dominic will be fine.'

'Success! That man will do anything for me.' Rita takes a gulp from the mug of strong brown tea which Philippa has placed by the phone. She swallows loudly.

'But don't you think he's sort of unpleasant?' says Philippa, sitting across from Rita at the other office desk, and gingerly picking over a pile of flaccid balloons.

'Not if you know how to handle him right,' says Rita. She looks at Philippa.

'Oh really?' says Philippa, selecting a pink balloon, pulling at it with her long thin fingers, tweaking it and stretching it.

'Yes, really,' says Rita, returning to the phone. She knows what this is about, of course. It's because Philippa wouldn't dare to promise, to flirt, to use her sex to get results. She's jealous, and Rita can't be doing with it.

'I won't have enough puff for all these,' Philippa then says. 'Mrs Swales, we need a hand-pump thingy.'

But Rita isn't listening. She's had enough. She's dialled home and is speaking to her husband, Collis. 'Darling,' she coos. 'Just to let you know. I got Ben to give your shoe a polish, it's in the hall.'

'Thank you. I've seen it.'

Collis's response is perfunctory, cool, and it pulls

Rita up. 'That's good,' she then says. Hesitantly.

'I nearly tripped over it,' Collis continues.

'You did?' Rita glances at Philippa.

'I did.'

Philippa's staring into space with the pink balloon, partially inflated, caught between her lips. It juts like a tongue stuck out to offend.

'Well, I told Ben to put it on the rack,' Rita continues, hoping her assistant isn't listening in.

'Well, he didn't put it on the rack,' Collis snaps.

'Didn't he?' Rita takes in a breath as Philippa releases one into her balloon. 'Well, will a new white shirt make up for it? There's one in the wardrobe. I thought you could wear it with the Paisley tie and those brown cufflinks that—'

'That go with my eyes,' Collis finishes. 'I know. Anything else?'

Rita watches the balloon suddenly fill, Philippa taking it from her mouth.

'Yes?' Collis asks.

'Well—' Rita wants to go on, to say, You could put on a happy face, stop blaming me, stop forcing me to tread on eggshells, stop pushing me because one day you'll push too far.

'Yes?' Collis repeats.

Philippa knots the balloon's end. She looks at Rita.

'Oh, nothing,' Rita replies.

The Beginning

Rita took her afternoon tea-break early and hurried to the cloakroom. She stripped off her McGee's overall and bundled it into her locker. Then she went to the toilet and checked herself in the mirror. As always her hair and face were frosted with fabric wisps. She picked off the largest but she still looked weird, as if she was wearing a shimmering caul. But there was nothing she could do about it. Only a thorough wash and shampoo would return her skin and bouffant to normal, and she hadn't the time or equipment for either. Rita had to trust that the schoolboy wouldn't notice or, if he did, that he wouldn't care.

She scurried from McGee's. Her break was almost over and what she was doing was risky. She could lose her job and so could Celia, who had promised to cover for her: 'Three-quarters-of-an-hour,' she'd said. 'Your break included. So, get moving, and don't do anything I wouldn't do!'

Rita hid beside one of the tall pillars which formed the entrance to Cranley's Industrial Laundry. She had a good view of the school and waited nervously, watching the first slow trickle of kids leaving for home.

Usually Rita didn't hang around for fellas. She didn't have to. There was a queue of them wanting to go out with her. Neighbours and workmates and frequenters of Scamps, her Saturday-night haunt. She could take her pick, except she was beginning to realise now they were all of a type. Men with no imagination, no fever, who, without exception, treated her as if she were the bee's knees yet took her along the same worn trail of seduction: the 'romantic stroll' beside the Crossforthian Stretch, the French kiss beneath the dripping wet arch of Iron Bridge, the request for sex while skimming stones across the smelly canal. Rita was ready for someone who might behave differently, who might offer something new, an uncharted land.

This boy.

Rita's heart was racing. She checked her watch and then looked up as a rush of pupils came through the open school gates. Their grey and purple uniforms blurred before her and she worried that she wouldn't recognise the boy in the scrum or that he wouldn't see her or worse that he would ignore her. But then there he was, calling, 'Hey!' and crossing the road towards her.

They ended up in a lane which looped round McGee's Fancy Underwear and ran behind some local shops. They were surrounded by dustbins and empty boxes, crates and polythene bags, which a sweet spring wind occasionally lifted into the air. The bags sounded like birds then, exotic birds with delicate wings.

'My name is Rita,' she said as she kissed him.

'Collis,' he replied.

Rita fingered the crotch of his grey school trousers. The boy was hard. 'Collis,' she said. 'Nice.'

A Request

Rita leaves the toilet, closing the door behind her, then she makes her way to the dinky black CD player fixed between two leaflet racks. She turns the player on, selects a CD, and inserts it. An airy seductive sound blows through the office. Rita wiggles her fulsome behind – twice to the left, twice to the right – and 'Party!' she chants. 'Party! Party!'

'Are you okay, Mrs Swales?' Philippa enquires.

'Yes, why shouldn't I be?' Rita's eyes are drawn to three breath-filled balloons which her assistant deftly bunches together. The balloons are shaped like tears and they glisten like tears.

'Your husband?' Philippa persists.

'What about him?' Rita asks. She stares at Philippa. So the girl *was* listening in, and now she's pretending concern when really she's still prying.

'Well,' Philippa braves. 'The call seemed very short.'

'That's because we didn't have much to say. Now.' Rita changes the subject. Emphatically. 'They're pretty.'

'Pardon?' Philippa looks at Rita.

'The balloons,' Rita replies. 'They're pretty. The pinky-mauves. We should make a feature of them. Any ideas?'

'Oh,' says Philippa, glancing at her bunch. 'Well—'

'Tape them to the filing cabinets?' Rita suggests. 'Or what? Come on Philippa.'

'Or...um—' Philippa flushes. Then. 'Or we could put them round the door, or the window. Or we could tack them to the ceiling. Or what about the partition? Yes. There's some mother-of-pearl and a very bright white. We could cover the partition in bands of colour. What about that, Mrs Swales?'

But Rita's attention has shifted. 'And where have you been?' Rita bellows at Nolene who's shouldering the agency door wide.

Nolene wears purple leggings and a black Lycra top and crimson lipstick which is too heavy for her teenage face. 'Mrs Swales,' she says, cheerily. 'I'm sorry I'm late but, look, I've been using my initiative.' She swings a carrier into the office.

'Your initiative!' thunders Rita.

'I've been to the chemist's,' Nolene continues proudly, unfazed. 'I've brought toothpicks and plasters and aspirins and Alka fizzy stuff and mouth freshener and these cute baby ice-packs.' Nolene briefly fishes in the bag before giving up. 'You know, you put them on your head if you have a blinder.'

'No one will get a hangover *during* the party, Nolene,' says Rita.

'Oh.' Nolene looks discouraged. 'They're probably a mistake then, but—' She rallies. 'I've got some Dettol, that's bound to come in handy.'

'Now, that is a good idea,' Rita grants. 'After the state you got in at New Year, with your head down the toilet, retching away. We had nothing for the smell.'

'I agree.' Philippa hurries to side with her boss. She grimaces, fanning the balloons about her screwed-up, protesting nose. 'It was foul.'

'Oh, they're nice,' Nolene suddenly remarks, her eyes fixing on the pinky-mauves.

'Indeed they are, Nolene, and guess what?' Rita says.

'What?' Nolene smiles.

'Get rid of the bag. I've a job for you.'

Rita continues with opening the mail. She examines the contents of each envelope before placing it on one of three piles: bills, monies received, miscellaneous. She slides a nail beneath the flap of the last envelope, the grubby specimen with a recycled label Sellotaped around it, and she pulls out a scrap of paper which is smeared with Biro splotches and fingermarks. She smiles. She knows what kind of a missive this is. A miscellaneous. A nutter's. A loony-toon's.

It's surprising the number of letters Rita gets from such people asking for jobs or, worse, threatening her, and at first she used to worry. But now Rita knows that basket-cases never follow through; she has yet to be bombed, stabbed, or set on fire; no certifiables have tried to cross her threshold or look her in the eye. As a result their crazy communications, their green-inked meanderings, have been stripped of menace, and Rita, regularly, unflinchingly, uses them for sport.

'Listen to this,' Rita says to the red-cheeked youngster who sits cross-legged on the agency floor surrounded by tear-, snake-, crescent moon-, black pudding-, and football-shaped balloons.

Nolene pulls a snaky one from between her lips and the air mewls out of it. 'What?' she gasps.

'Shush. Listen.' Rita holds the letter high. 'I've found just the man for you.' And begins to read the spidery handwriting in a creeping nasal whine.

Dear Rita's Housesitting Service,
All that is mine I carry with me, my coat and bag are my home. I sleep under the big wide sky. I toilet in public conveniences ... under archways and bridges, and sometimes – if I am taken short – shop doorways...

'So that's what the awful pong was by the step,' comments Philippa, standing on a chair near the partition, and tacking-up the first wave of balloons. 'He's been round already.' The inflated pearlised rubber glimmers, sending out sparkly seeds of light while capturing the yellow blocks of summer sunshine pressing thickly through the agency's front window and door.

'Might've been a dog,' Nolene mumbles.

And Rita reads on.

... I am oppressed by roots, permanence, fixtures, fittings.

My childhood was spent with an angry mother and a distracted father ...

Philippa gets down off her chair. 'Oh, but that's sad.'

'Weird,' says Nolene.

...We lived in a vicarage...

'Weirder,' says Nolene.

... It was brutally clean. It stank of displeasure. I left as soon as I could, absconded to enjoy the earth, the stars, the sea with its lovely lapping – what a generous sound ...

'He's quite poetic,' Philippa concedes. She is now on the floor beside Nolene, and Nolene hands her an inflatable which is an anomaly, a vile maroon cucumber, a tube of ugly blood.

> *... But I am getting old now: my bones seize with the frost. I need a little shelter. Four weeks a year, in the winter, to recharge my batteries. That should be sufficient...*

'He's educated,' Philippa says, rejecting the balloon, aiming it at a wastepaper basket.

> *... I'll drop by soon to see if you can offer me this. Do not be afraid. I am decent. I shave and have a woman who is crazy enough about me to wash my smalls...*

Rita laughs – 'dirty devil' – and balls up the letter, before finishing,

> *...Yours,*
> *Edward Pearson.*

'Well, what do you think, Nolene?' Rita asks. 'Is *he* your type?'

'I don't have a type,' says Nolene.

'You don't have a man,' Rita replies.

'Neither does Philippa.'

'That's because I'm fussy,' Philippa rejoins.

'Besides,' Nolene continues, pulling at her top, sliding her fingers around the inside of the turtle-neck. 'I might not want one.'

'Honestly, Nolene,' Rita then says. 'Have you no brains? You're cooking in that. Black in this weather.' Rita pats her warm broad hands down the front of her own summery blouse. 'You won't last.'

'Sorry,' says Nolene.

'Well, why don't you finish the balloons and then go

home and change into something more suitable and while you are out in the big wide world you can collect my party frock from the cleaners? It'll be ready at eleven. Okay?'

'Okay,' Nolene smiles. 'Thanks.'

'And, let's see, a few other things too. Take a couple of tenners from the petty cash and get a big plastic-thing of milk, some toilet paper, some washing-up pads, a box of household matches ...'

Nolene's smile begins to fade.

'And this month's *Domicile* and *Property Pavilion* ...'

Nolene stares at her feet.

'And a couple of pairs of tights,' finishes Rita.

'Tights?' Philippa enquires.

'Someone's bound to get a ladder this evening.'

'And then we can come to the rescue.' Philippa looks startled. 'That's inspired, Mrs Swales.'

'I know.' Rita is pleased with herself. 'Now, you'll manage all that, won't you, Nolene?'

'I suppose so,' the junior mumbles.

A Decision

Rita and Collis couldn't keep their hands off each other, but it was difficult because they had no place to go to. Collis's parents liked Rita and welcomed her into their home but Collis had three brothers and there was no privacy. There was Rita's parents' house but Rita and Collis only managed to sneak up to her bedroom once before they were banned.

Rita's parents had smelt the couple's desire and believed it to be unhealthy, disgusting, wrong. A twenty-year-old with a fifteen-year-old. It had nauseated them, and Ernest had called Rita a tart, a cradle-snatcher. 'I could get you prosecuted,' he'd shouted, and his threat had pursued Rita and Collis like a vicious little dog.

So they made do. Sometimes they used the toilets in Scamps or the allotment sheds on Crossforth's only stretch of green. But mostly the couple used:

Celia's brother's car on Tuesday nights.

Rita – though she didn't yet have a licence and drove badly – used to take the silver Cortina to Greenacres, the poshest area in Cranley, parking it down one of the long, empty driveways or in the bowl of a secluded cul-de-sac. It was often dark, after nine, but she and Collis barely glanced at the stars. Because the stars were nothing compared to clambering over the gearstick and handbrake and through to the back seat, pulling up jumpers, pulling down pants, coming so wildly that Rita would yowl and bash her head on the window winder – once or twice the knob of the handle meeting her brow, wounding her. 'Oh my God. Oh my God,' she'd cry and Greenacres – a sound sleeper, it seemed, with no worries – never woke, never stirred.

Celia's place – or technically her boyfriend's – on Thursday nights.

Celia had dumped the crane-driver and was going out with his supervisor instead. The supervisor had more money, he had his own flat, and he was besotted with Celia. He'd do anything for her which was why he agreed – when Celia asked – to let Rita and Collis use his bachelor-pad.

This arrangement lasted a year – fifty-two nights in a double bed with silky black sheets – until Celia two-timed the supervisor with a butcher and got found out.

The Coach and Horses on Saturday afternoons.

Occasionally, Collis and Rita paid for an afternoon in room 48B on the third floor of the no-star Coach and Horses, a pit-stop for travelling salesmen, located in the centre of Cranley.

The Coach and Horses was managed by Mrs Ethel Cram, a blowzy woman who had earned a frightening reputation in Crossforth before moving to the hotel. She was huge, her breasts and belly were one ginormous heap, and – it was rumoured – a man could get lost in her flesh should he dare to board her; and – it was rumoured – she invited many a man to risk it.

Ethel Cram used to live round the corner from Rita's parents' house, and had once accosted Ernest on his way home from work. What passed between them was never revealed to Rita, the details of the transaction were never disclosed, though Rita could still recall her father closing the front door with shaking hands, then letting go with curse upon curse in the living room. He railed against Ethel. He called her scum. And then he let it all unravel: his loathing for Crossforth with its flotsam and jetsam, his loathing for the District Council and its inept building-work, the damp in the extension, the relentless grey sky which darkened the relentless grey streets, the stink exuding from the turbid canal. Rita and her mother listened helplessly, then Rita's mother tearfully whispered, 'She's not worth getting so worked up over, Ernest. She's dirt. She's filthy dirt.'

Collis felt contempt for Ethel too. He was young but he wasn't wishy-washy, and Rita liked this about him, though sometimes she wished he'd bend a little and, as far as Ethel was concerned, feel grateful.

'She's one of the rare ones,' Rita argued. 'She doesn't condemn us.'

'Well, how can she?' Collis replied. 'She behaves far worse. Besides, she's not going to say anything, not while we keep paying.'

'Afternoon.' Mrs Ethel Cram's voice was lost beneath the jingling of a brass bell. The bell sounded whenever a person stepped in or out of the Coach and Horses. It was fixed on a bracket above the door and was the brightest item in the establishment. Rita and Collis often caught Mrs Cram standing on a stool, at full stretch, rubbing the bell with a Brasso-soaked duster, her exertions causing her skirt to rise high, displaying her awesome thighs.

'Fond of that, isn't she?' Collis would say. He believed Ethel would burnish a strip of fly-paper if it enabled her to flash. 'There's more on offer here than polyester sheets and a five-bob breakfast,' he'd say.

'You've no proof,' Rita limply defended. 'The bell could have sentimental value. A gift from her mother.'

'Or a regular,' Collis replied.

Rita crossed the hotel lobby and Collis followed. It was always like this. Collis annoyingly lagging behind, refusing to link arms with Rita, to touch her in Mrs Cram's presence. 'Hello,' said Rita. 'Nice day.'

'Oh yes,' Ethel smiled. She lounged (her weight disallowing a more decent posture) on the reception desk, and the desk, made of thin plywood sheeted with Formica, creaked and wobbled beneath her meaty arms.

Rita placed her handbag on a corner of the desk. She clicked the bag open and rummaged in it for her purse. 'Well here we are again,' she said brightly, compensating for Collis's sullenness.

Mrs Cram smiled some more. '48B, and something else?' she asked, directing the latter part of this question to Collis.

Collis turned to peer through the uncurtained lobby window. 'Um, yes,' Rita hurriedly answered. 'The extra, please.'

'Fine.' Mrs Cram took a set of keys from the keyboard, then bent, huffing and puffing, to produce a small package from under the desk. She presented it to Rita.

'Thank you.' Rita gave Mrs Cram a note from her purse and gathered up the keys and the package, feeling the boxes of three through the brown paper wrapping. Rita's doctor had refused to prescribe Rita contraceptives – 'Not until you are married, I'm afraid' – and sooner than face other medics whose responses would possibly be less kind, or have Collis frequent the barber's too often (his hair was so short now people were asking him if he'd enlisted) Rita had approached Ethel.

'There's a little surprise for you,' confided Ethel. 'A present from one of our lorry drivers. They're foreign. From Paris. They feel very different. No extra charge.' She counted Rita's change on to the desk.

Rita slid it into her purse. 'Thank you,' she murmured.

Rita and Collis lay on their backs facing the ceiling of room 48B. It was painted orange-brown, like everything else: the walls, the carpet, the furniture, even the bedsheets in 48B were orange-brown. It was tacky and dismal and they couldn't help but find it depressing.

Collis turned on his side to look at Rita. He ran a thick finger along the curve of her waist, out over the rounded hump of one buttock, and Rita smiled.

'I hate that woman,' Collis said.

'I know,' Rita replied. 'But don't let Ethel spoil things. Don't let her spoil this.'

Rita touched his face. His skin was smooth and babyish, his chin dotted with dark bristles which weren't stubbly or manly – not yet. Collis was still a kid. He was out of school now and working but he was still a kid. A very beautiful kid who had been surprisingly innocent when she'd first met him, not as sexually confident as his poise had suggested. In fact, she'd had better. But strangely it hadn't mattered, because Rita knew Collis would improve, because from the start there had been something more to him and her.

There was the third party.

Love.

Rita was sure.

A sheltering, protecting, all-encompassing bubble of

love, which lifted Rita, raised her above Crossforth's greyness and grime, McGee's and the sameness of her days there.

Happily-given love. Never-ever received from Agnes and Ernest. Unconditional. Honest. Not blind.

Collis nudged a fingertip into Rita's crack. Rita felt the stubby nail press against her and she moved to meet it, to follow its circling.

'We need to go,' said Collis. He nodded at Countdown Charlie – the clock he always brought with him – on the bedside cabinet. Countdown had a round plain dial and was made of blue painted metal. A basic clock with a conscientious tick. A reminder that Rita's and Collis's time was limited, that this nest of dreary orange-brown was theirs for five hours only. Tick. Tick. Tick. It was a sound which threaded through their love-making, occasionally causing it to become desperate, only half an hour to go, fifteen minutes, thirty seconds. Tick. Tick. A sound which so irritated Rita that once she'd hurled Countdown against the wall, denting his crown. And now the damage was dressed with a plaster. Collis's doing. His joke.

'It's nearly six,' persisted Collis.

'Pull your finger out then.'

'What, and put this in instead?' Collis's cock was hard again. He pressed it teasingly against Rita's thigh.

'A quick one,' said Rita.

'A very quick one.'

Rita took Collis's cock in one hand and with the other searched under the pillow for a rubber.

'We should get married,' Collis said, kissing Rita's breasts, licking her nipples. 'Then we wouldn't have to deal with her, we wouldn't have to make do.'

'Shush,' said Rita. 'Here it is.' She passed the sealed packet to Collis. 'We've gone over this. Marriage isn't possible, not yet.' She stroked Collis's balls as he ripped the packet open. 'My parents wouldn't approve. It would get too horrible. We have to wait, win them round.'

'I'm fed up waiting.'

'I know.'

'We shouldn't fucking have to.'

Suddenly Collis chucked the condom at the wastepaper basket. It missed, and landed slackly on the orange-brown carpet.

'Collis!' said Rita. 'We need that.'

'No, we don't.' Collis got up and put the rubber in the basket. 'We don't need that.' The basket was also orange-brown. The room number was taped to it and the written instruction: *Discard all sanitary wear here. Ladies will be fined if they cause a blockage in the toilets.* Collis returned to the bed.

Rita felt something lurching in her stomach. 'Oh,' she uttered.

'Yes.' Collis was calmer now. He'd decided. 'Come on, Rita. We've talked about it. We know we want a baby and it'll sort your parents out. They'll be begging us to get hitched. It's a good idea.'

'Oh,' said Rita again.

Bill

I love the woman. I love the woman. I love the woman. Rita Swales has it all for me. I can't be doing with young pieces, silly girls.

I was married for twenty years before my wife left me. She went off with a college lecturer. She was doing a 'refresher course' to boost her confidence. She was a mum for too long, she said, and this man – he knew what he was doing – he charmed her with fancy talk. He wooed my wife with impressive words. 'Motivation,' he said. 'Inequality.' Then he drew up my wife's CV, and he turned her head, and I had to let her go. I couldn't do a thing about it and I was a mess for months afterwards. I missed her. I missed what she'd grown into, her maturity.

I love mature women, which is why I fell for Rita Swales. When she set up her agency next-door. Well! She dresses smart, she's a good-looker, but she can't hide what she's lived through. I wanted her from the off. The way she moves. Her belly. Her thighs. She's got a rear to die for, and her tits are weighty; and I couldn't believe it, back there in the stockroom that time, when she allowed me, when she asked me to hold them. They had the heaviness of everything. Time. Her hard chunky teats. And now I'm desperate. I want more. When I see Rita Swales I want more. I love her. I want to grab her and take her.

But it's not just her flesh. It's everything about her. I look at Rita Swales and I see sex and I see stature. She is magnificent. She's struggled and she's bigger because of it. She's dragged herself up.

She started Rita's Housesitting Service with no experience, with only 'a feel for homes', that's what she told me. She was waiting her turn at the dentist's and she read a piece in a mag and she thought, 'I can do that. I have a feel for homes. I know everything there is to know about homes.' Can you believe it? Such courage. Such a jump in the dark. And she pulled it off. She's like I imagine my wife to be now. A blinding success.

But of course Rita Swales has her sons and she has her husband. Nothing's ever simple is it? She's married to a man she can't leave because it would look too bad, and Collis would never leave her because he hasn't got the guts, because Rita's his crutch. And I wouldn't like to wreck a family, not even if I could. But I'm torn. I love the woman. I do. I really feel for Rita. And carrying on as we are is seriously screwing me up.

The End

The wedding was held in Cranley's Registry Office, a monstrous round-shouldered building which loomed over the neighbouring fish and meat market and Cranley Bus Station, gorging on their noisome emissions. The raw flesh and petrol stench lingered in the Registry's foyer like persistent halitosis. Most brides passed through quickly, keeping their coats buttoned tight over their flouncy princess gowns until safely ensconced in the sluiced and swilled betrothal suite at the building's rear.

Rita, though, welcomed the pong. It was animal and heady and precisely matched her wedding-day mood. She strode through the foyer proud and erect, decked only in crocheted trousers and a lacy top. She carried a posy of violets which she clutched high against her pregnant belly. She felt ripe. She tingled all over with a thick woozy tingle which was almost turning her inside-out to reveal her hot pumping heart, her desire for Collis, her longing to be Mrs Swales.

The ceremony was simple and quick. They had few

guests; Collis's parents and siblings, Rita's parents (her father in the suit he usually reserved for funerals) and Celia. It was intimate, intense. Collis's hands shook as they exchanged the rings, and Rita wept.

The party stood on the Registry's steps, Rita and Collis on the lowest, the rest behind, and the air hung thick and reeky around them.

'You're going to have to squeeze up. I can't fit you all in.' Celia tottered on her high-heels, crouching and swaying before the party, a pocket-sized camera (borrowed from her current beau) held to her face.

'We are squeezed up.' Rita laughed, laying her head on her husband's shoulder.

'Well, hello, Mrs Swales,' Collis whispered.

'Well, hello,' Rita replied, as their baby flipped inside her. 'Here.' Rita took Collis's hand with the gold band shiny on his ring finger and placed it on her domed belly. 'Someone's happy.'

'Me.' Collis smiled. 'I am.'

'Look. Blast. I'm sorry. I won't be a minute. This doesn't seem to be working.' Celia shook the camera and prodded its viewfinder.

'Let me help,' offered Tony, one of Collis's brothers. He joined Celia, edging close to her powder-pink suit, her pale powdered skin, her hair in long loose ringlets.

'He'd better watch out,' Rita told Collis. 'She'll have him for breakfast.'

'That's what he's after.' Collis moved his hand over Rita's belly, running his thumb along the weighty droop of her breasts. 'I love you, Mrs Swales.'

'I love you too,' Rita replied.

'Good.' Collis brushed his thumb across her nipples. 'I'm glad.'

'And I will always love you.' Rita was melting. 'And I will never ever leave you.'

'Bugger that!'

Ernest was directly behind Rita and she felt his sudden expletive jab at her neck. Bridling, she turned to face him.

'Don't.' Collis said. 'Forget it. Celia's ready.'

'Well, she'll have to wait now.' Rita glowered at her father. He was skinny, agitated, flanked by the rounder, stiller presences of Collis's mother and Rita's own.

'Yes, too right,' Ernest barked, pulling at his carnation buttonhole, tugging it from his lapel. 'She'll have to wait now because I can't be doing with this, this *blessed* carry-on.'

'What carry-on?' Rita challenged.

'You, with your belly out to there, in front of that camera. You should be ashamed. You needn't think I'm going to stand here and be part of it—' Ernest threw down the carnation.

'Ernest, for once in your life—' Collis warned.

'Don't you lecture me, son,' Ernest snapped, pushing past Agnes, stomping off.

'Mum!' Rita looked at her mother, but Agnes was in no state to act, to call him back.

Agnes hadn't congratulated Rita and Collis when they'd told her of the pregnancy and their intention to wed. She'd not said anything. But her body had stiffened, and she'd kept this carriage throughout the preparations and now into the day. She'd sat in the Registry, in the first row of a five-row block of high-backed wooden chairs, with her gloved hands clasped in her lap. And she'd stared past the marrying couple at the vase of creamy-yellow flowers on the table next to the celebrant.

Rita had noticed the gloves most of all. Her mother had bought them especially. They were an unblemished white but they made Rita think of muck and mess because they extended beyond Agnes's wrists and they had a scalloped edge like her orange washing-up gloves.

Rita could imagine Agnes's fingers inside them itching to get scrubbing and rubbing, to erase, to wipe clean every tarnished and spoilt thing – her life, Rita's life – about her.

'Mum?' Rita's baby stopped its flipping. It slumped in the bowl of Rita's womb as Rita watched the dewy tears fall, unchecked, down Agnes's big blank face.

'Just leave me be, Rita,' Agnes said.

Rita lay on the hospital bed, an old bed made from metal tubing. It was functional, austere. The mattress was hard and aggravated Rita's pains. The porter had laid her on her back, and a nurse had slipped a depleted pillow under her head. She couldn't move, she had no strength. She couldn't even get her fingers to undo the ties of her hospital gown: the strips of fabric had been knotted and each one pressed into her spine like a knuckle. It was miserable. Her whole body ached, her legs felt as if they'd been crushed, her vagina and anus were burning and wet. A whiff of something horribly pulpy and bloodied was coming from under the bedsheet.

It was mid-morning, autumn. A golden sun shone through the ward windows. Rita felt its warmth on her face, it stroked her closed eyelids, and she supposed she should be grateful. She supposed the sun was trying to tell her this – be thankful, you got through it, you're alive, you are alive. But it was still too fresh, the pain, the shock of her body being taken over and mangled. She couldn't be appreciative. No way. She couldn't open her arms and embrace the world or her baby. She felt angry and cheated. Why hadn't anybody told her? Why did they let her go in there thinking it would be wonderful? Why weren't they honest?

'Mrs Swales?' someone whispered. A woman. A nurse. Rita registered the papery rustle of uniform, but refused to respond. She wasn't ready to converse, to share. She pretended she hadn't woken.

The nurse moved closer, placed a hand on Rita's swollen breasts. Rita flinched. She'd been given an injection to suppress her milk, but it didn't seem to be working. Her breasts were huge. They felt like plum tomatoes dropped in boiling water, puffed scarlet and bursting through their skin. The nurse patted them briskly.

'Bugger off!' snapped Rita. 'Christ!'

The nurse removed her hand – 'A little tender, Mrs Swales?' – then squatted to look in Rita's face. 'Your baby's been checked,' she persisted. 'He's fine, and we'll be bringing him for Mummy to cuddle and feed. A bottle has been made.'

'I'm too tired,' said Rita. 'I won't treat him right.'

Collis came at visiting time in the evening. The nurses had propped Rita up in bed. They'd arranged a couple of pillows behind her back and had run a comb through her hair. Just before Collis was due they'd formed Rita's arms into a cradle and balanced her baby there. Rita's arms sagged with the child's weight but she didn't complain, she didn't beg for her first-born to be taken from her as she'd done earlier. She just sat, holding the bundle in front of her like she was waiting for the rag-and-bone man with an unwanted pile of clothes.

Collis walked up the ward. Rita watched him. She watched how sturdy his body was, how perfect. She didn't think it was fair, him remaining so beautiful, so unscarred. His life hadn't been touched. He'd barely been affected.

He wasn't present at the birth – he hadn't been allowed. He had sat outside in the waiting room looking at the clock, drinking strong tea and looking at the clock. And when it had reached seven-thirty he'd gone to work, because he had no leave to spare, none to spend with his labouring wife.

Rita watched Collis walk up the ward. She watched his body, his face. She loved him and she hated him. He could've phoned in sick, lied to his boss, and stayed around. Rita had wanted him to. She'd wanted him to be there for her. When they'd wheeled her and the baby out of the labour suite, she'd asked for him. 'Collis?' she'd whispered weepily to the nurses. 'Where is Collis?'

'Shush, Mrs Swales. No crying. He's gone to work. He'll be back later.'

'Bloody hell, Rita,' Collis said, as he drew up a chair. He sat down. He hadn't washed, there was a smell of factory about him, and his hairline and fingernails were dirty. 'You look terrible.'

'Thanks,' said Rita. 'Had a nice day?'

Collis shook his head. He observed Rita. 'Too tired and too busy thinking about you,' he replied, his confidence faltering. He glanced down, began to twiddle his fingers, pick the muck from under his nails. His eyes avoided the baby.

'It was like shitting a brick,' said Rita, wanting to make him squirm, to make him pay. 'A breeze block, one of those big grey ones with the jaggy edges. I'm ripped up.'

'I'm sorry,' said Collis.

56

Doreen

Mrs Swales can be rather overwhelming but she's kind too. She's been very kind to me.

When I left school I went to work on a fish stall in Cranley's fish and meat market. I loved it, I had my very own apron and special responsibility for crustaceans. But then my father fell ill – he was deeply depressed, I suppose mentally sick – and my mother couldn't cope. She ran away and so I had to give up my job to care for my Dad. I looked after him nineteen years until he died. It wasn't very pleasant and it didn't help me to be indoors all that time, it turned me in on myself. I was terrible at the funeral. I cried and cried but the tears weren't for him: I was on my own and I had no money, and I didn't know what I was going to do. I'm ashamed of how I behaved then. I was a wreck and Mrs Swales saved me.

The Job Centre showed me her ad and told me to apply. They said it was either that or lose my benefit. Then Mrs Swales called me for an interview and I was so nervous but she made me a cup of coffee and said, 'I'm not going to shoot you, Doreen.' It surprised me. It calmed me down. My mother and father both used to play mind-games with me, pretending not to have said stuff when they had, screaming they loved me as they hit me. But Mrs Swales gave it straight. I know where I am with her. She calls a fish a fish. This can shake you sometimes, but mostly I find it a relief.

'You'll suit the work, Doreen,' she said to me. 'We don't want flashy characters. We want people who have an affinity for homes.'

'I wouldn't be without mine,' I replied. My voice was becoming hoarse. I was out of the habit of speaking in long sentences. 'It's all I have.'

I've never looked back, though sitting can be hard. You get rotten customers, and it's terrible if a water-tank bursts, or the drains block, or the client's weeping willow is set alight by a next-door neighbour bearing a grudge, as happened to me last summer. But Mrs Swales has always been there for me. She's never threatened the sack. She's snapped at me but, as I say, you know where you are with her, and I think that's special.

Business people usually succeed by being sly, by not caring for their employees. But Mrs Swales isn't like that. She succeeds because she is good. A good person, who is good at everything.

A Woman in Need

Rita rubs her hands over her rump, and makes soft patting movements as she looks at the clock above the agency door. It is eleven. She has half an hour before her appointment with Mr Arnold, and wonders what she can squeeze into the time. She turns abruptly and makes for the loo, where she collects a half-filled watering can. 'You're doing very well,' she says to Philippa on her return.

Philippa has covered the partition with balloons and is now looping streamers across the office ceiling and over the walls. She is balanced precariously on the edge of her desk, standing with paper-chains clutched in her hands and twisted round her ankles, a row of tacks clenched tight in her mouth. She can only manage a nod in response, and Rita smiles. 'Good girl,' she says. 'Take a tea-break when you've finished.'

Rita kneels on the sofa and leans over the back to soak the fern. The plant is thirsty, its roots poke from dry, crusty compost, and its thin thorned branches are an insipid green. It cannot cope with the summer heat, and quivers feverishly as it sucks up its drink.

Rita wants to swap the fern for a plastic version, but Celia won't let her. 'Artificial foliage is crass,' she informs Rita. 'Very unchic.' But Rita is unconvinced. She feels sure an inanimate plant of regular colour and unchanging height and width would be more attractive than this shabby, unpredictable item. She leans further to empty the dregs from the can, and the grateful greenery embraces her with its fronds. 'Oh bugger,' she hisses as she finds herself ensnared.

The agency door opens. Rita hears someone step inside. She agitates to free her hair, but it's no good. 'Philippa! Philippa!' she calls.

'Mmm,' replies Philippa, vigorously rustling. Rita's assistant is evidently still bound by bunting, and Rita tries not to panic. What to do?

'How's things then?' says the visitor. Her voice is familiar.

'Josie!' A relieved Rita lets herself dangle. 'Come over here woman, and cut me loose!'

'Well!' Rita stands to smooth her blow-wave. 'That Triffid is *out*.'

'Oh no, Mrs Swales,' says Philippa, escaping her own fetters and clambering off the desk with some urgency. She has a multicoloured streamer wrapped around her head, eco warrior-like, a rainbow tribeswoman. 'That fern's a feature,' she defends.

'But they can give you awful rashes.' Josie slides on to the couch. 'And they drop their dead feathery bits all over the carpet. I mean, it's a mess back there.'

Josie is a bedraggled-looking woman. She dresses cheaply. Today she sports a pair of baggy purple shorts, a Take Five Video Store baseball cap (her uniform) and a pink cheesecloth blouse. She has gathered and tied her blouse in a knot below her bra line, leaving on display a strip of pale flesh and a sticky-out belly button shaped like a snip of dowelling.

Rita eyes the belly button. She is fond of Josie but is troubled by her style. It reminds Rita of how she used to dress when she was young, a knackered mother short of cash and time. Rather sniffily she says, 'It's a mess everywhere, Josie, as you can see, because we are trying to get ready for this evening. Also, I've an appointment soon so I can't stop to chat.'

'Oh.' Josie removes her baseball cap and uncurls her long, lank pony-tail. 'I forgot all about the party. In fact, I was hoping you wouldn't be busy, because—'

'Because?'

'Oh, I don't know Rita. I just don't know any more, I just—' And then, wide-eyed, as if startling herself, Josie begins to cry.

Rita sits at the office computer, attempting to compose a quick reply to a client's letter, attempting to ignore Josie who's holed-up in the staff quarters, but she can't. The woman's sobs are loud and her rattling cup and saucer are noisier still, the chink chink chink adding a manic edge to Rita's ambience music.

Rita sighs. Why are cuppas always given to people to calm them? The drink may be soothing, but the crockery is like a transmitter, turning horribly audible the sufferer's nervousness, anxiety, feverish sorrow. Rita walks over to her player and ejects the CD. She then puts her thumbs in her ears and considers an alternative.

She could burn scented oils or joss-sticks. The hippy stuff would be quieter and she knows the smell can pacify. Her second youngest imbibes and he drips around their home like a tranquillised housewife. He drives Rita nuts. But perhaps in her office the sandalwood stink would come into its own.

Rita unplugs her ears. Briefly she imagines silence,

but then her ears pop and – clink clinkity clink – Josie is still at it. Rita yanks the partition open as far as the balloons will allow. 'Hush! Please!'

Philippa is crouched in front of the fridge. She ineffectually clutches a box of tissues. 'I'm sorry Mrs Swales,' she says. 'I can't do a thing with her.'

Josie swallows a sob. 'It's not my fault,' she gulps, slumped on a chair by the sink. 'I don't want to be like this.'

'Well,' Rita suggests. 'Why don't you put your cup on the drainer, and wipe your eyes and nose? Your nostrils are bubbling. And you, Philippa, go hold the fort.' 61

Rita swaps places with Philippa who gives her the tissue box and whispers as she edges past, her dainty chest brushing Rita's more buoyant bosoms, 'She didn't want me, Mrs Swales. She wants you because she says you'll understand.'

'Oh really.' Rita looms over Josie. She takes the cup from her jittery hands, replacing it with a man-sized three-ply. 'Get wiping,' she orders.

Josie pushes the tissue round her face, roughly dabbing her eyes. Then she thrusts it at her nose and blows. Her blow activates her legs and one pale thigh swings skinnily over the other. 'Bill shouldn't have bollocked me about the computer,' she complains. 'I was doing fine till then. But he was so nasty and it was too much, too much on top of everything else.'

Rita leans against the fridge. She could do without this. She has suffered enough aggro for a Monday morning already. First Doreen. Then Derek. And Collis. Now Josie. She folds her arms, fingering the HRT patch on her left shoulder. She'll need to replace it soon. She mustn't forget or else she'll be having a dizzy spell or worse a prickly heat will grip her limbs.

Josie snivels, and Rita looks from Josie's unhappy,

fretful face to Josie's dirty trainers to her own strappy sandals and shapely feet and her nails painted with red varnish which are visible through her fine stockings, and she wiggles her toes. It's no good. She might as well get on with it, hurry it up before Mr Arnold arrives.

'Is it your ex? Has he been bothering you again?' Rita asks. She nods towards Josie's injury – the scarlet snarl of shrivelled skin flaring from Josie's right knee to the hem of her shorts.

'In a way.' Josie dabs her eyes, the tattoo *S 4 J* visible on her pinkie. 'He's been given a council flat on Rosary Road. His girlfriend is expecting. It would be okay except he's still down as leasing tenant at ours.'

'And that's a problem?' prompts Rita. She moves from the fridge, closer to the partition opening.

'Of course it is,' Josie replies as Rita peers through to her office. 'He's got another council place and he shouldn't have, he's not allowed two, and so me and Angie – his own daughter, his flesh and blood – have got to evict. A fortnight. The Council has given us a fortnight. Rita, are you listening?'

Rita's office is quiet; sunlight glistens on the glossy green paintwork making it appear tropical, luscious; Philippa is sitting at the office computer perhaps spell-checking – as she is inclined to do – the letter Rita was working on; and the agency clock points to eleven-thirty. Oh shit. Mr Arnold is due. Now. Rita sees a man walking towards the agency door. It could be him.

'Sorry,' says Rita, turning to face Josie. 'You'll need to go. I'm expecting my client any second, and Bill will be wondering where you are. It wouldn't do to lose your job as well as your home, would it?'

Josie looks at Rita. She appears surprised. 'Bu—' she blurts before slumping over. She hugs her stomach, then starts to sob again.

Christ Almighty. Rita crouches. She cups her wide

hands over Josie's knees and jiggles them furiously. She doesn't know what she's doing, she just wants Josie to shush.

'I c ... c ... an't cope,' howls Josie.

'Shush,' says Rita. She hugs Josie to her chest, pats her hair, her shoulders. 'Shush,' she repeats, feeling something slimy drop between her breasts.

Snot!

Rita's toddlers used to rub their noses on her, daubing her with gooey streaks, the tacky tattoos of motherhood, the bogey badges of weariness, responsibility and unsexiness. Rita thought she was past all that. She *is* past all that. Forcefully, she pushes Josie away.

'Ow!' Josie's head jerks back and hits the sink unit. She whimpers. 'I don't want to be homeless. I don't want to be jobless.' She sniffs and rubs her nose across her knuckles.

Rita watches her coolly. She hasn't time for other people's traumas, not any more. She is busy, and besides, who was there for her when she needed help? 'Then fight,' she tells Josie. 'You'll get nowhere in this world if you don't fight. There's no use blubbing.'

The video-store assistant takes her baseball cap off her lap. She picks at the stitching which runs round its peak. She locates a loose thread and tugs it. She continues to make sorrowful noises. 'I know that, Rita,' she moans. 'It's just—' But Rita has turned away from her.

'You'll have to excuse me, Josie,' says Rita distantly, hearing the agency door open, the draught excluder brush the floor matting. 'But I think this is my client.'

Rita hurries first into the toilet cubicle to check her face in the mirror. She looks good despite everything, pink but not sweatily so. She licks a finger and dabs it on her eyelids, smoothing her make-up, the soft cream shadow which has turned a little motley in the heat. She pushes her hair into shape, removes a stray sprig of fern, then dries her cleavage with toilet paper.

Rita smiles at Josie as she leaves the cubicle but the smile is hard, bright and breezy, painted on in readiness for her appointment. 'Use the back door, Josie,' smiles Rita. 'The key is on the fridge.' She moves to the partition and Philippa is there to meet her.

'Mr Arnold,' whispers the assistant.

'Thank you,' says Rita. 'Now, can you put the kettle on and make Josie disappear?'

'Of course, Mrs Swales,' says Philippa.

'And do it without letting her start up again? I don't want any more tears in the office, it's hardly good practice.'

'I know, Mrs Swales,' Philippa sighs. 'I know.'

Rita inserts another CD in her machine, calming herself, breathing deeply, then she turns and jauntily walks towards the tall man. 'Mr Arnold is it?' He stands by the agency door, sunlight showering through its glass panel, framing his body. It gives him a movie star look, a charismatic aura.

'Rita Swales,' he says, his voice charming, intimate. He offers a broad hand and Rita takes it, feeling lively blood dash through her veins, with a rhythm as gay and seductive as the music now swirling round her office.

'Indeed,' she says, and gives a happy laugh, pressing her palm into his, warming to his grip. His knuckles are hairy and she feels this manliness with her finger tips. Mmm. She is going to enjoy herself, she can tell. Mr Arnold is her kind of client.

A Man Indeed

Rita stands close to Mr Arnold. She has explained about the party decorations, that the agency is celebrating its fifth anniversary today, and now she shows him her certificates, her framed documents of achievement. She points out her Small Business Enterprise Awards, her *Service-With-A-Smile* runner-up shield, her Associated Tourist Industry *Most Successful Innovative Venture* gong for 1994.

'Very impressive,' comments Mr Arnold.

Rita smiles. 'Very well-deserved,' she says. She studies Mr Arnold's linen suit, the cut accentuating his broad shoulders and chest.

'I know so.' Mr Arnold looks from Rita's accolades to Rita herself. His eyes skim her face and settle on her plump breasts, her heavenly cleavage. He smiles too. 'You come highly recommended, which is why I'm here.'

Philippa places a cup of coffee on Rita's desk and a plate of ginger creams. 'Thank you, Philippa,' says Rita, sitting in her shiny silver chair and crossing her legs. 'If you can work through your in-tray and have your break when I'm free again?'

'Certainly, Mrs Swales,' says Philippa, with a glance at the client.

Mr Arnold, who sits opposite Rita on the other side of her desk, smiles at the assistant. The smile is asexual, non-encroaching, different to the one he flashed at Rita. It is the kind of smile which Philippa, Rita knows, warms to.

'Thank you, Philippa,' says Rita, wanting to shoo the girl away before she embarrasses herself.

But Philippa lingers. 'Shouldn't I get on with the profiles?' she says, glancing once more at Mr Arnold.

'No.' Rita is brusque. The profiles are a grievance. They shouldn't be raised now.

'Oh.' Philippa runs a hand through her hair.

'I need to check the files first.' Rita stresses. 'And I won't be doing that, not while Mr Arnold is here.'

Mr Arnold regards Philippa with a steady gaze. She blushes. 'Oh, no, of course. I'm sorry.'

Rita pushes the drink and biscuits over to Mr Arnold. She waits for Philippa to return to her desk and sit. 'Ah!' Then she raises her voice. 'I'm afraid my assistant's forgotten the sugar.'

'Oh.' Philippa gets up. 'Sorry.'

'Do you take sugar, Mr Arnold?' Rita sweetly asks her client.

'I gave up sugar when I gave up my wife,' he replies.

Rita smiles at Philippa as she hurries from the staff quarters with the golden granulated. 'Back you go,' she says. 'You're saved. Mr Arnold isn't a sugar fiend.'

'I'm partial to these though.' Mr Arnold reaches for a ginger cream – 'May I?' – and briskly bites into it.

'So you're separated?' Rita ventures, feeling the pulse in her wrist palpitate. 'You live alone then? This is something we do need to know.' She rummages in a filing tray on her desk, and removes an orange folder. The words – *CLIENT DETAILS: Intro/1* – are printed on its front. She flips it open and takes out a three-page pink form interleaved with carbon.

'No human companions now,' says Mr Arnold. 'Fortunately or unfortunately. But I do have an aquarium, a well stocked aquarium. I've a *penchant*, a *tendance* for tropical fish – Blue Acaras, Clown Loaches, Angelfish, Flying Foxes...'

'What lovely names!' exclaims Rita.

'Whiptail Catfish, Pearl Danios...' an encouraged Mr Arnold continues as Rita takes a pen from a green desk-tidy which nestles close to the filing tray. 'Leopard Danios—' Rita clicks the pen to release its ball-point.

'So exotic,' she interjects. 'Obviously, you'll need a sitter who can care for them.'

'Obviously.' Mr Arnold takes a gulp of coffee and Rita eyes his Adam's apple as it moves chunkily up and down. 'My fish are important to me.'

'Well, it shouldn't be a problem,' smiles Rita. She positions the pink form directly before her, smoothes its pages, and writes her initials and the date in the top right-hand corner. She continues, 'I know two of my sitters are acquainted with fish: Keith Wellington, an ex-biology teacher, is an enthusiast, and Doreen Abbs used to work closely with marine life. But perhaps what we should do is fill out one of these forms.' Rita taps the document before her.

Mr Arnold looks intently at Rita. His eyes are a deep brown, and they remind Rita of her husband's eyes: so dark they don't reveal anything, so dark you can barely distinguish the black dot of pupil; very disconcerting eyes; eyes which can make you angry, or – Rita reaches for the handbag which rests against her feet – *hot*.

'Excuse me,' she says, unzipping the bag and delving

deep for her small battery-operated fan. She locates its slim plastic body and pulls its helicopter-shaped blades free from a tangle of lipsticks, cotton-wool balls, and handcream. She switches it on and runs it around her face and chest and upper arms. 'It's getting quite warm in here,' she says.

Mr Arnold blinks his brown eyes. 'You should open a window.'

'Sealed fast,' explains Rita. 'Security.'

Rita offers the fan to Mr Arnold. He mouths a 'thank you' and holds it to his shirt front. The striped-cotton fabric flutters delicately.

'Now,' says Rita. 'Completing this won't commit you to anything, but the information you give will enable us to formulate a service package. The package will be uniquely tailored to your needs and will be outlined in a comprehensive report which we'll send to you first-class tomorrow. The report, which is free-of-charge, will also include details of costs, insurance requirements, a draft contract and sitter profiles. If you commit yourself to using the agency within fourteen days of receiving the report then we will give you a 10 per cent discount on your first two sits. Obviously you can phone or drop by if you have a query. But if you commit, and we hope you will, then we can arrange another meeting to go over any outstanding items and to fix dates for your inaugural sit. Shall we begin?'

Rita works through the form slowly. She starts with general personal details: name, address, telephone number. She uses a low, coaxing voice to request the information and Mr Arnold leans forward, holds the fan whirringly between them, and willingly responds. He watches Rita as she writes his replies on the pink questionnaire.

Rita's handwriting is strong and curvy. Her 'y's have lively tails, the crosses of her 't's are long and bold and slice through other tall-stemmed letters, her 'b's have big pregnant bellies. It is a confident style, it has a happy sensual rhythm.

The first page is done in five minutes, then Rita relinquishes her pen to flip to the next. She runs her hands along the edges of the document to get the carbon and top copies in line. She takes a deep breath and informs Mr Arnold that she is about to ask more intimate questions, and he should be assured that his answers will be treated in strictest confidence. She clears her throat.

Would you prefer your Housesitter to be male/female/either?

Male, because men are less inquisitive and more practical.

Can the sitter bring a companion along – a friend/partner/relative/pet?

No, I want my sitter to be looking out for my home, not for any*thing* or any*body* else.

Would you prefer a non-smoker?

Yes, I can't abide smoke. It discolours the paintwork and its smell clings to curtains and carpets.

You would prohibit cigarettes. Is there anything else?

Drugs. Alcohol. Chocolate. Access to my office and library, my bedroom and bathroom *en suite*, the contents of my freezer.

I also have two large Persian rugs – they are situated in the drawing room on the ground floor – they are decorative features and are not for walking on, the sitter should tread round them at all times.

Please describe your home. What size is it? How many floors does it have? Is it well-kept?

It is a three-storey Victorian house, across the road from this agency. It is immaculate. I employ a cleaner three days a week, Monday, Wednesday and Friday mornings, seven to eleven.

Is there anything in your home which will require special care in your absence – pets/plants/dependants? (We have sitters who are qualified to look after elderly relatives and young children, but we charge a higher rate for their services.)

My fish, for which I will supply detailed instructions. They are on a strict regulated diet and it must be adhered to.

I have houseplants, but they are made from silk.

I have no dependants.

Do you have a garden? We will not weed, dig or plant, but we will water if necessary.

My garden has been tarmacked.

Do you have any alarms?

I have a security and fire alarm system which needs to be checked at least once a week.

Will any other persons have access to your home during your absence?

My cleaner and nobody else, though my ex-wife may try to gain entry. Please contact the police if she does, she is under a restraining order and is forbidden to approach me or my property. I will provide photographs.

What three words come into your mind when you think about your home?

Castle. Important. Territory.

What three words come into your mind when you think about a sitter living in your home?

Trepidation. Necessary. Trust.

If your house caught fire what three valuables would you want saving first?

Filing cabinet. Fish tank. Persian rugs.

Rita shakes Mr Arnold's hand, then guides him across the office, past Philippa who glances up shyly from her hunched position at the computer, and towards the door.

She swings her ample behind so it knocks once or twice against his sculpted thighs, and she talks as she walks, pretending she's unaware of their touching, and her heart flickers, enjoying the game.

She has secured him, she knows, because she rarely fails with the men. They respond well to her and she to them. They appreciate her professionalism, but more, they are persuaded by her looks, her charm. A little flirting can go a long way and, with some men, that's all it takes: a heave of Rita's bosoms and they willingly entrust their homes to her. It is as if they are wooing Rita, gifting her, so she may show them more attention, think well of them, fall in love with them.

It is never so easy with the women. If a man attends with his wife or girlfriend, then Rita will cut the flirting, or only flirt when the woman is in the toilet, examining a leaflet or rummaging around in her handbag for her list of questions. There is always a list of questions. Rita will be less forward but she will not shift her focus from the man.

Because women, Rita has found, are cautious and clingy, clutching their homes to their skirts like mothers holding on to toddlers, their own flesh-and-blood. Many bring photos of their house's exterior or their favourite rooms and they show these to Rita, explaining what they have invested in the property – the emotional and material investment, the amount of hours and love. Rita has even seen women cry, suddenly splinter at the idea of entrusting their *Dunroamin* or *Cozy Cottage* to a stranger; worse, to another woman. Rita has heard the words 'desertion' and 'never forgive myself' and 'tearing me apart'. It is no fun and it is draining, and Rita is never sure she has managed to convince them of the virtues and trustworthiness of her business. She is never as sure as she is when interviewing a man. Never certain she has won them over.

Rita wonders if she should delegate the women to Philippa. Rita has noticed that they respond better to Philippa's Sunday School manner, her flat chest and dulcet tones; and Rita knows Philippa welcomes responsibility. Nolene is a straight nine-to-five girl with no ambitions and she is very young, but Philippa likes to be challenged and to be seen to succeed. Rita makes a mental note to ask her, as she opens the agency door wide.

'Goodness!' she exclaims as her flesh meets the hot air outside. It is humid and thick and reeks of tarmac. It has muscles. Rita can feel it pressing upon her and pushing past her, hungrily mingling with the stuffy closeness of her office. She is almost beaten by the brew and has to resist the urge to slump to the ground, to succumb to it.

Mr Arnold lingers over her. 'You have been very helpful,' he says.

'Thank you,' Rita murmurs. She eases the door back with her body to make a gap for Mr Arnold to step through.

He edges by as a welcome breeze comes in from the street to ruffle his hair and lift the fabric of Rita's blouse. The straps of her bra are revealed and the lacy scooped edge of one creamy cup. Mr Arnold coughs and runs a finger round the neck of his shirt, releasing a smell of sweet aftershave and spicy sweat. 'And you will be in touch?' he asks.

'In touch, yes.' Rita smiles. 'Your report will be sent to you first-class tomorrow. Or, if you prefer, it could be hand-delivered, since you're just over the road.' She smoothes her blouse, and her golden bangles jingle.

'Yes, excellent,' says Mr Arnold, stepping from the threshold. 'I hope your party goes well.'

'Thank you,' calls Rita. 'It starts at five. In fact you're

quite welcome to come along. Since you *are* just over the road.'

'Perhaps I will,' he says.

Rita watches Mr Arnold walk to the kerb. He moves very precisely, like aristocratic beefcake, his buttocks knitted together, his shoulders square. Rita briefly admires his frame as he stops and checks the road for traffic. Then she looks away to the faint heat-haze which swims across the far end of the street.

The haze is soft-hued, yellow and pink, and people wander in and out of it. They appear semi-transparent, like apparitions, like figures moving easily from one world into another, from way back then to now.

Tired and Achy

Rita crouched over whingy, wriggly Jimmy. She moved her head from side to side and goggled her eyes, making a silly face to distract him. A large nappy-pin was clasped between her teeth and she had one hand pressed on Jimmy's chest to keep him fixed to the settee. With the other hand she attempted to fold the terry triangle around his Vaseline-shiny backside.

She was hot. She was boiling with the exertion and frustration. Why was it always the same? Why – when she had plans, when she was short for time – did Jimmy play up? And why wasn't he so badly behaved with his father? If Collis needed Jimmy changed and dressed in a hurry then Jimmy would be sweet-as-pie, compliant and floppy.

'Bugger it!' Rita spat out the pin, spraying squirmy Jimmy with her saliva. She let go of the terry and whammed his chest with her hand, winding him, freezing him, his plump wobbly limbs stiffening. Jimmy blinked at her. He couldn't understand and he was frightened. Rita could see this in his baby eyes but she didn't want to care.

'I don't care,' she told her second son. 'It's your fault. You're such a bloody fidget. Now, will you keep still?'

Rita scurried round the flat. 'Excuse Graham, excuse,' she said to her eldest who was toddling now and keen on pursuing her closely. '*Excuse!*' Rita shook herself free of him and dashed between the four rooms – from the bathroom to the bedroom to the kitchen to the living room – gathering things for the trip and cursing as she did so. She hated the flat. It was too small. She was forever bashing herself against its walls and doors, tripping over furniture and now Graham, who was a living breathing unrestrainable obstacle (unless Rita dumped him in his cot, which she was doing far too often).

Collis had chosen the flat. It was situated two streets from Cranley Bus Station and they were renting it privately. They'd thought about putting their names down for a place in the twin towers in Crossforth, perhaps staying with Celia – because Agnes and Ernest wouldn't have them – until the building work was finished and they could move in. But neither of them could face the prospect. 'We need to get away,' Collis had said. 'A fresh start. It doesn't suit us, Rita. We, you deserve better.'

And he'd been right, and in the beginning the flat had felt ideal. It had seemed big and pleasant and had smelt of freedom. Collis had lifted the pregnant Rita over its threshold and carefully twirled her around the tatty, badly-decorated rooms and she'd squealed. Delighted. It had felt so good to have escaped, to be free of the Devices, of her pinched parents and their pinched and pokey terrace.

'And here's the kitchen,' Collis had shouted. Light had flowed through the dust-filmed window to glaze the front of a unit, the stainless-steel sink, the white electric cooker, and it had looked so glittery and hopeful that Rita suddenly burst into tears.

Collis laughed, holding her, rocking her. 'Why the tears, daft bat?' he'd soothed. 'Why the tears?'

'This is what I've been waiting for,' Rita had sobbed. 'This is what I've always wanted.'

But now it felt as compressed and as cluttered as her old home. The kids had to have so many things: cots, changing stuff, a steriliser and bottles and tins of milk powder and baby food, and clothes, and toys. Their arrival and accompanying paraphernalia had shrunk the space, and there wasn't a garden, not even a yard, for them to spill into. No fenced-in safe spot which would give them a breath of air, the chance to ignore each other, and the chance for Rita to unwind. Because she needed to unwind.

'*Stop it!*' Graham was tugging at Rita's tracksuit bottoms and she gave him a kick to make him let go. He tumbled on his back and she quickly scooped him up to prevent him bawling.

'Now.' She put him near the front door. 'You sit there,' she said, buttoning his cardigan and putting on his harness. She clipped reins to the harness, then wrapped the reins around the door handle, securing him tight. 'While I collect your brother.'

Rita strung her plastic shopping bag – heavy and chocker with stuff – over her arm and she bent carefully to lift Jimmy off the settee. 'That's it, no wriggling. I've got lots to carry,' she said, as she held him against her shoulder, taking a last look around the flat before leaving.

She checked the cooker was switched off and the windows were shut, and she flushed the toilet, grimacing at herself in the bathroom mirror as she did so. She looked dreadful. Her hair had been hacked and tinted by one of the cheapest stylists in town and stuck up as if she'd slept on it badly (heavily and uninterrupted, she should be so lucky). She couldn't do a thing with it and she was going to meet Celia and was worried about her reaction, would her friend gasp or giggle at the cut? Rita hoped she would be kind.

She opened the front door. The flat was above a lock-up and the way out was down a steep flight of stairs. When Rita was feeding Jimmy late at night, she often heard chains being yanked from the lock-up's wooden door and a lorry reversing to dump a load. Occasionally, she fretted about what was in there, but the landlord wouldn't elaborate on, 'Storage, my dear, storage. A few odds and sods, that's all'. More often Rita felt too tired to care.

The stairs exacerbated her tiredness. Most days she couldn't face them and stayed indoors, plonking the kids and herself in front of the telly. Some days though she just had to get out. She unwound Graham's reins and manoeuvred him on to the top step. He clutched at her leg. 'Mind,' she warned.

Jimmy kicked his muscular feet in response to Rita's voice. 'Mind!' she said again as they descended. 'Careful please.' Jimmy's feet knocked the shopping-bag, and it began to swing.

'Jesus! Jimmy!' cried Rita. She rammed her shoulder quickly against the wall, struggling to stop herself from toppling forwards, from letting go of her sons. 'Christ,' she hissed, watching plastic pants, a milk bottle, baby spoon and baby bowl, bolt from the bag to clatter past a wailing Graham, ricocheting down.

Wholesome and Bright

'So, what time shall I order the taxi for?' The telephone receiver is cold against Rita's warm neck.

Collis yawns. 'I'll leave that to you,' he replies.

'You have a choice,' Rita persists, wishing she could have avoided calling him again. Normally, when Collis is in one of his moods, she steers clear, but today is different. Everyone will expect him to be at her do, by her side, supporting her, celebrating with her. So she has to keep in touch, to ensure he'll turn up. 'You can arrive before the party starts, or a little bit into it, or—'

'You know best.'

'But I don't. Look—' Rita pauses. She must tread carefully, because Collis can be pushed the other way. 'If you arrive early you'll get a seat.'

'Mmm.'

He can get angry. He can drop his distance and launch into a diatribe, an unwelcome blast of complaints and more self-pity; and then there'll be no coaxing him round.

'Shall I do that then, order the taxi for half four?'

'Mmm.' Collis yawns again.

'Are you tired?' Rita tries to sound concerned, not irritated. 'Did I wake you earlier?'

'No,' Collis replies. 'You didn't wake me.'

'Well, why not take a nap? You don't want to be yawning at the do. And I'll phone you back this afternoon with the taxi details.'

'Fine.'

'Fine.'

Rita replaces the receiver. She sighs and looks over at Philippa. Her assistant is peering too intently at the computer screen. Her cheeks are flushed, and Rita realises she's been earwigging again. 'Philippa!'

Philippa turns to face Rita. 'Yes, Mrs Swales?'

Rita stares at her assistant. 'Those profiles?' she then asks, watching Philippa shift uncomfortably in her chair, her face registering confusion. 'What's the problem?' Sometimes it pays to skip the expected reprimand, to behave contrarily, thus keeping the employee on her toes. 'You'll have to remind me.'

'Oh.' Philippa shakes her head. 'The profiles.' Getting herself together. 'Yes, well, I'm worried about them.'

'You're worried about them?'

'Yes, Mrs Swales. I'm worried I won't get them to the printer's on time. I really need you to go through the records. Please can—'

'Well, good morning! Good morning!'

Philippa and Rita look from each other towards a peacock's fan of flowers that is striding over the agency threshold on a pair of tracksuited legs and flat pumps.

'Well, good morning!' says Rita.

'Floral Desires making a delivery to a Miss Rita Swales,' the huge bouquet announces.

'Mrs,' Rita corrects. Then. 'We'll have to talk later,' she says to Philippa before opening her arms to receive the awesome display of roses and carnations. What a tonic! Just what she needs. Though she knows they're not from her difficult husband or even from an admirer, that she's ordered them herself.

'Mrs,' says the bouquet, dropping forward to reveal a rotund delivery-woman smiling beatifically. She has a scrubbed face and heavy eyebrows. Her hair sits on her head like a joke-shop toupée.

Rita thinks Happy-Clappy Wholesome-and-Bright, and tries not to smirk. 'And the rest?'

'In the van,' Wholesome-and-Bright replies. 'I could do with a hand. There's a few buckets.'

'I expect you could.' Rita places the bouquet on her desk and stands. 'Well come and help us, Philippa!' she shouts. 'Chop! Chop!'

'It's all looking very jolly,' says the delivery-woman as she walks to her vehicle which is parked, with hazard lights flashing, outside Take Five Video Store.

'Yes,' Rita replies, following behind. She glances at the store and spies Bill. He holds a fluorescent yellow poster advertising 'EX-VIDEO RENTALS FOR SALE.' Rita waves as he sticks the poster on to Take Five's window. Bill mouths something like, 'Hello, Gorgeous,' and blows a kiss. 'But,' Rita smiles tinglingly, 'It's only supposed to be a small affair and I'm beginning to wonder whether I've gone a little over the top.'

The enthusiastic representative of Floral Desires opens the back doors of her mini van and leaps into it. Rita spies a 'V' of sweat staining the seat of her ill-fitting trackpants. 'What's it in aid of?' the woman asks, while Rita presses her hands under her own armpits, checking for and not wanting to find similar patches, because visible perspiration isn't kosher in her line of work.

'The agency's fifth anniversary,' says Philippa,

appearing beside Rita, who has just discovered the effectiveness of her Dual (dries and scents in one easy action) Deodorant.

'Well, I'm sure it's going to be wonderful,' the delivery-woman chirps, handing Philippa the first bucket. She then jumps from the van and fusses with the blooms, standing a few stems upright and removing a dead-head. 'Off you go now,' she says to Philippa.

'And for me?' Rita asks.

'Won't be a minute.' The delivery-woman drags a large pail of greenery from the van's interior. The agency phone rings.

'Christ!' The word slips from Rita before she can do anything about it.

'Language!' Happy-Clappy chastises, thrusting the pail at Rita.

'Oh!' Rita grabs the dirty bucket before it meets with her blouse. She hears the water slop around inside it and she hears the answerphone click on. Where's Philippa? Rita makes for her agency, walking as quickly as she can, trying not to upset her liquid cargo. The machine will give the caller the wrong impression, that the office is closed, that it isn't revving and ready to party.

Rita's father's voice greets her as she steps over the threshold, and Rita immediately relaxes. Ah, thank goodness, it's only him.

'Sorry,' says Philippa, coming from the staff quarters. 'I was—'

'Shush,' says Rita. 'Let me listen.'

Ernest's voice is feeble, shrunk to the size of the little black machine on Rita's desk. Rita gives her pail to Philippa, catching the mossy smell of the departing greenery, and she smiles.

'Rita? Are you there? Are you there, Rita? It's your dad. Can you pick up the phone?' Rita shakes her head. Ernest pauses, and she hears him breathing, his wispy breaths. He is on his way out and Rita imagines she will be arranging his funeral soon, this winter perhaps, or next spring. He will be put in the plot beside her mother and his name will be added under hers on the plain grey headstone. Rita looks up at the balloons tacked to the partition, and the streamers looped across the office ceiling and walls, and she listens.

'You're not there, you'll be busy. Well, I was just wondering if you could bring me another video? When you visit. If you've time. But not like the last one, if that's okay? Something with a bit of action. In English, if you can. Car chases. That'd be good. Okay, Rita? If you can.' Ernest pauses again. 'Thank you.'

Rita looks at Philippa.

'He likes his videos,' Philippa says.

'Yes,' Rita glances at the clock above the agency door. 'He does.' It is nearly dinner-time. She pictures Bill's wide leathered hands firming the yellow poster against Take Five's window, and she decides she is due a break. 'Well, it looks like I'm going to have to go on an errand,' she says merrily. 'And I'll get a bite to eat too, while I'm out. Won't be long, you can cover, and when I come back I'll see about the profiles.'

'Thank you, Mrs Swales.' Philippa hurriedly gathers some carnations from her bucket and a sprig of green from Rita's. 'But before you go.' She wraps a sheaf of A4 round the dripping-wet stems, and she hands the improvised bunch to her employer. 'You *could* give these to Josie,' she suggests. 'I'm sure she'd appreciate them.'

'Yes,' says Rita, taking the blooms. 'That might be an idea. Thank you, Philippa.'

Rita grabs her bag and jacket from the staff quarters and leaves the agency. She is immediately faced with Happy-Clappy who has two buckets tucked under her arms and an invoice clamped between her teeth. The delivery-woman moves her head from side to side, waggling the invoice, drawing attention to it.

'My assistant will see to that,' Rita graciously responds.

Something Rotten

Though the towpath had been tarted up, the canal itself remained sludgy and smelly. It was early afternoon and the hot sun was drawing a blue vapour from the murky surface. Flies clustered – dark shifting pools – in the spoilt air. Rita could smell shit, the high whine of excreta.

She halted the pram to pull the sheet across her children's noses. They were both asleep, thank God, snuggled up together. Jimmy was still, but Graham wriggled, balling the linen in his chubby hands, and so Rita rolled him on to his side, turning his back to the stench. She stuck a dummy in his mouth and hoped that would be enough to keep him content, to keep him from waking and yawning, gulping up the pong.

A hedge of conifers grew on the land-side of the path, blocking Rita's view of Crossforth and the twin high-rises, the pink and the blue towers where her parents and Celia now lived. But even so, she could still feel the Devices, waiting for her, over there, tugging her in. She wished she didn't have to come.

Above the entrance to the blue tower was a plaque bearing the name *Speedwell.* A smaller plaque, an architectural award (runner-up in the *Best Use Of Limited Space* category), was fixed beneath. Rita held the entrance door ajar with her buttocks and, with a sigh, pulled the pram inside.

The tower's interior was painted the same blue as the exterior, but a mosaic brightened its first fathom, a depiction of sea creatures and shells and a sunken galleon which undulated across the lift doors to lick at the stairs. It was so un-Crossforth, except for the accompanying atmosphere, a sour moistness which complemented the oceanic scene. Damp. A reminder of the terraces, a legacy. Rita looked at the mound of mosaic tiles by the lift doors, the seascape pitted with hollows of greeny-black perspiring plaster, and she sighed again.

Rita rang her parents' bell, and rocked the pram as she waited for someone to answer. 'Oh,' her father said on opening the door. 'It's you.'

'Yes,' Rita replied.

Ernest was wearing his check workshirt, the sleeves rolled up to reveal his wiry arms and, on his left wrist, his ancient, battered Timex. Rita backed the pram past him, biting her tongue. He'd asked for a digital watch from Rita's catalogue for his birthday, and Rita was paying it off still at eighty-five pence a week, and yet she only ever saw him sporting this old one.

'Hair's a bit of a mess, Rita,' he observed, shutting the door decisively behind them.

'Thank you,' said Rita, as her mother came from the kitchen, wiping her hands on a tea-towel.

Agnes pushed the towel into her housecoat pocket and leaned over to look in the pram. Graham and Jimmy were still asleep. 'Ah, bless them,' she said.

'Well, they might be little darlings now.' Rita pulled

her shopping-bag from the wire tray beneath the pram and gave it to her mother. 'But they certainly weren't earlier. Graham's into everything.'

'Yes,' said Agnes indulgently, picking through the items in the bag. 'But I expect we'll manage.' She took out Jimmy's drinking bottle. There was a line of dried milk by the bottle's neck and Rita – knowing it wouldn't escape her mother – winced on seeing it.

Rita's father switched on the telly in the living room, then returned to the hall. He stood next to Agnes, working his hands round the waistband of his trousers, tucking his shirt in. He appraised Rita as he hoicked up his pants, and fiddled with the crotch. Rita averted her eyes, and saw her mother homing in on the milk mark, rubbing it with her thumb. 'Seems to be on the inside,' Agnes remarked to Rita. 'Did you bring a bottle brush?'

Ernest looked at Rita's hair. 'Who did that then? Was she wearing dark glasses? Did she have a white stick?'

Rita said to her mother, 'No, sorry, I didn't.' And, then, unable to stop herself, she patted and fluffed her hair, as if trying to recover its previous shape.

'You can use the mirror in the bathroom, Rita,' Agnes offered, placing the shopping-bag by her feet, then poking a pinkie into the bottle to get at the stain. 'If you want.'

'Too late now,' said Rita's father. He made for the living room. 'I can't understand it,' he called. 'You and Celia used to be such a pair, and now look at you. You're letting the side down.'

'She has two children, Ernest,' Rita's mother defended.

'Yes,' said Rita. She stared through the doorway at her father and he gave her a wink from his armchair, a slow shutting of one eyelid, and Rita turned her back to him, feeling useless. She so wanted to keep away from the Devices but couldn't because she needed a babyminder. And she so wanted to keep away from Ernest but couldn't because her parents were a package, they didn't come separately. And if Rita stopped seeing Ernest then she'd have to stop seeing Agnes too and then she'd lose her babyminder, the only babyminder she had.

'Rita will be her old self once the kids start school. You'll see,' Agnes continued.

'I hope so,' Rita said.

'Pull the other one.' Ernest's voice was braying, and it woke Graham.

The toddler spat out his dummy and began to whimper and wriggle. His fists were knotted in the sheet and he struggled to free them, his efforts causing his mewls to change pitch, to harden into a wail. 'Bugger,' snapped Rita, seeing one of his chubby arms flop out and hit his brother in the face. Jimmy's eyes flicked open and then he too raged.

Ernest turned up the sound on the television. The buzz of racing cars zooming round a circuit filled the hall. Rita closed the door on the racket, on her father, while Agnes bent to comfort the children, her pallid scalp visible between the strands of her fine grey hair. 'Thanks, Mum,' Rita murmured, backing from the flat.

Something Light

On sunny days the Kopper Kettle spilled on to the city centre street. Mrs Sinclair (the manageress who wore a black beret and took her holidays, she said, in Montmartre, Paris) dotted metal chairs and tables pierced with parasols along the pavement and employed extra staff to waitress. Then, the place seemed bright and cheerful and welcoming. But come the bad weather – like the summer downpour which was just visiting – the furniture and checked tablecloths and vases crammed with imitation flowers were stashed in the back and the café retreated inwards, taking on a gloomier aspect. Rita splashed over its threshold and was swamped by a fug of cigarette smoke, and the smell of fried bread and holed-up humans.

The place was busy with thick-set mothers supping strong tea and their tiny children drinking Tizer; a few lonesome males occupied the high stools next to the counter and listlessly stirred mugs of milky coffee. The only free table was near the toilet. Rita pushed her shopping beneath it and sat down.

Celia joined her. She dropped her bags. 'Can you sort these?' she asked. 'And make the order? Mine's a weak tea and custard slice. I've got to go. I'm busting.'

Rita ran her hand through her wet hair and bit into her cake. The synthetic cream oozed from the éclair and drew a moustache on her top lip. She licked it off as Celia came from the loo.

'Well Miss Swish,' Rita greeted. 'Who's been treating you?'

Celia removed her new slim-fitting camel jacket and draped it over her chair-back. She sat down and unwound the green silky scarf from her neck. She smiled. 'An admirer,' she said, patting her long hair which was sleek with rain and not frizzing like Rita's.

'It can't be James. He hasn't got any money,' Rita continued, feeling the distance between them, how little they now shared. She'd sunk into soiled nappies and drudgery, Celia was still working, single and kid-free, and their relationship had changed, become unbalanced, like everything else, tilted against her. Rita chewed on her éclair.

'You're right!' Celia congratulated. 'It's not James. It's somebody new.'

'I can't keep up with you,' Rita mumbled.

'I know,' Celia said, warming her hands on her tea cup. 'Isn't it dreadful?'

Rita nodded, because it *was* dreadful, it was enviable how Celia got through her men. Over the last six months alone Celia had flitted to and from:

The next-door neighbour.

A lanky bachelor who Celia had seduced on Day One of moving into her flat in Speedwell. But the sex had been feeble. 'He needed a lot of coaxing,' she told Rita. 'His mother had just died.' A two-night stand, though he continued to give Celia pieces of his mother's jewellery, rings and brooches which he'd press shakily into her hands.

The policeman.

Celia had worn his uniform in bed and, yes, she joked, his truncheon came in handy.

The twins.

Brothers from Crossforth's roughest family, nephews of Mrs Ethel Cram. They'd wanted to take Celia together but she'd made them visit on alternate nights. She'd preferred the one with the birthmark on his neck. 'He had a way with words,' she told Rita. 'He could talk dirty.' He still phoned her occasionally to whisper a few filthy nothings.

The policeman.

The same. Celia had returned to him for four weeks. She was partial to his truncheon and, more, the police station bar with its fancy cocktails and complimentary ploughmen's.

The dustman.

A squat bloke who'd flung Celia over his shoulder like a bin needing emptying, twirling her, making her cry, 'Stop. Stop.' Then, 'No. Carry on. Yes. This. Carry on,' as he lay her on her bed. A decent man who Celia might have loved for longer except he'd been going through a crisis which was visible, distorting his face with ticks and twitches. Like the neighbour, he had to go.

The newsagent.

A mistake. He'd had newsprint on his fingers and a squeaky voice. But at least he'd cancelled Celia's paper bill, and, now they were finished, continued to give her freebies. 'Here you are, duck,' he'd say, tucking a *Woman's Weekly* into her bag. 'Some nice knitting patterns in there.'

The policeman.

One night for nostalgia's sake. Another mistake.

The lift engineer.

An afternoon of ascending and descending. 'Going down,' he'd cried.

The know-all.

James who'd been sharing Celia's flat for a month. Penniless, but into books. He was handsome and his hands clasped cutlery and mugs and his books almost tenderly, wishingly. But he was too keen on imparting his knowledge and once or twice Rita had caught Celia grimacing at something he'd said, or looking at him blankly, uncomprehendingly.

'Yes, dreadful.' Celia sighed, and with her nail-varnished fingers dropped two sugar cubes into her tea. 'But tell me about you, Rita. What does Collis think of your hair?'

'He hasn't said anything,' Rita mumbled through the wodge of choux pastry churning in her mouth. 'I don't think he's even noticed and I'm glad because it's such a mess.'

'Oh I don't know,' Celia replied, raising her cup to stare at the dish-watery drink inside. 'It was brave of you. I'd like to go for something shorter but Simon won't let me.'

'Simon?'

'My new man.' Celia leaned forward conspiratorially and then she let go like she always did, reeling off the details, basking, flush with her success. 'He's a bank manager! He's got black hair, big hands and a lovely body. He lives in Greenacres.' Celia widened her eyes. 'He wants me to move in with him,' she whispered and somehow squealed simultaneously. 'Only trouble is, he's married.'

Josie

There's not much I can say about Rita Swales. There's not much I want to say about her. We get on okay and then she pulls rank. She puts on airs, and it pisses me off. Because we're the same, we've come from the same place. She's as common as I am but pretends she's something else, more than me, better than me. Simply because she got lucky.

I think there's something sad about her actually. She's play-acting. I feel that about her. She doesn't really know who she is. She parades round that office of hers, wearing her posh clothes and bossing her silly girls (I can't stand that Philippa one. She's precious. She's got no idea. I could kill myself crying in front of her). Then she comes on to my boss and he falls for it because, like a lot of men, he can't see through her show. And she is showy, all the time. And I think when somebody's behaving like that there can't be much underneath, or if there is, then it's a muddle, a mess. I think Rita Swales is a mess.

But then I suppose I'm no better than Bill, my boss. I'm drawn to her, I can't keep away from her. I shouldn't have gone to see her today. She humiliated me. I was hoping for understanding but I should've known Rita Swales wouldn't want to be reminded of hard times, bad knocks. I should've known she'd be cold.

She used to live not far from me. Her name was Myhill then, Rita Myhill. I'm much younger than her but I can remember seeing her about. I told Bill this when we were tidying the stockroom together. He's a stupid but decent man. He mouths off but he can be kind. My daughter thinks he's great, tells me I could do worse, which I have. But Bill isn't interested. He's not interested in me like he's interested in Rita. He listened to my story about Rita Myhill and Crossforth – about how she and her best mate took their men down the Crossforthian Stretch, snogged them beneath the Iron Bridge, surrounded by all that shit, pong and sludge – and he couldn't get enough of it. He didn't want to know about my life there, he just wanted to know about hers. It's always about her and it's sickening.

But I can't and I won't waste my time over Mrs (yes, she is a Mrs, and she shouldn't forget it) Swales. I've got real problems to deal with. My daughter doesn't want to leave her home you know. She likes it. It might not be in Rita Swales's class, but my daughter likes it.

Popping In

Rita puts her shoulder to the door of Take Five Video Store and pushes. The door resists, then swings open so speedily that Rita loses her balance. She topples into the shop, barely able to keep upright on the spiky heels of her sandals. 'Christ Bill,' she shouts, clasping Josie's bouquet to her chest with one hand while trying to save herself with the other.

Rita grabs a rack crammed with horror films but her legs are buckling and she crumples to the floor, hungrily pursued by *A Werewolf Came To My Dinner-Party And Ate Two Of My Guests!* This, the most hotly-rated video in the Lycanthrope Top Ten, clonks Rita on the back. 'Oh for fuck's *sake* !' she explodes.

'You all right, Rita?' Bill asks.

She remains slumped on the floor, burying her head in the flowers, sniffing them, trying to calm herself, counting to ten. She feels Bill's loafers against her buttocks.

'Need any help, madam?'

'Maybe.' Rita snootily raises an arm for Bill to take

and registers – on her journey skyward – a ghoulish face, lots of putrefying flesh. The poster reminds Rita of Stevie Richmond and all the other ugly mugs she has entertained for the good of her agency. This has a salutary effect. This and being vertical once more. A composed Rita frees herself from Bill and runs a hand through her hair. Her bracelets play about her wrist, jingling prettily.

'My kind of humour,' Bill says.

'What is?'

'Slapstick.'

'Ha. Ha.' Rita replies. She glances down at the flowers.

'It swells in the heat,' he reveals.

'Sorry?' Rita says.

'The door swells in the heat, and jams. Can't do anything about it.' The video store boss bends to pick up *A Werewolf Came To My Dinner-Party!* 'So what can I do you for?' he then asks.

Rita is cool. 'Your stock lowers the tone,' she says. 'It isn't in keeping with the neighbourhood.'

'Does well, that one.' Bill returns the film to the shelf, then moves closer to Rita, chancing to touch her, sliding a warm finger under her bracelets. He strokes her skin, briefly. 'This neighbourhood is not what it seems.'

Rita watches his face. 'What about my flowers?' she ventures, melting. 'Do you like them?'

'I like what's behind the flowers,' Bill declares. Rita's tremendous breasts. Animate like two jelly sea-creatures. 'Very much.'

'They're for Josie,' Rita persists. 'She's going through a bad patch.'

'You don't say.'

Bill glances down the aisle to his unhappy assistant, who is drooping over the service counter. 'Pull yourself together woman,' he shouts before turning back to Rita. 'Look, have you got time for lunch? Can you come for lunch?'

Rita smiles. 'Perhaps, but I need to find a video for my father first. He wants a car chase.'

'With sex or without sex? Before, during or after?'

'With sex but after. I think he'd want to see the chase first.'

'He likes a chase?' Bill smiles too.

'Yes, he does.'

Josie ducks as Rita makes for the counter. Josie ducks, then resurfaces with a can of Mr Sheen and a J-Cloth. She squirts the Mr Sheen high into the air, then sets about polishing the till like crazy, rubbing the key-pads so hard that *No sale*, *Transaction Void*, *Refund*, and the figures *9*, *99*, *999* flash across the display panel.

'Stop that Josie,' Rita orders. 'I've got something for you.' Rita places the bouquet on the counter, and scent puffs from the flower-heads to merge with the Mr Sheen. A sickly perfume. Rita coughs. Josie coughs. Their coughs crackle like mini lightning stalks and Rita can sense a charge in the atmosphere. A volatile charge, not as promising or as stimulating as the spark which passes always between Rita and Bill.

'What are these in aid of?' asks Josie, fingering the soggy sheet of A4 wrapped round the flowers' stems and glancing down the aisle at her boss.

'They're a good-luck gift,' Rita replies, following Josie's gaze. 'Good luck with the Council.'

Josie pulls a petal off one of the flowers. She examines it closely. 'I'm going to need it,' she says.

'Yes,' Rita mumbles, leaving Josie. 'I expect you will.'

Rita strides quickly down the aisle. She reaches Bill and stops, her sandals almost touching his toecaps, the width of a video – the car-chase video – between their bodies. 'I don't think Josie likes me today,' she confides.

'Josie doesn't like anyone today,' Bill confirms. He shifts his voice up a notch so his beleaguered assistant can hear. 'Do you, moany? I say, you don't like anybody today?'

'It's not my fault,' snaps Josie.

Rita takes Bill's arm. 'Come on,' she says, pulling him from his shop, and abandoning Josie who is now slumped over the till, her J-Cloth dangling limply like a flag begging surrender. 'I need food.'

Chickening Out

Rita wheeled the pram along Greenacres' main artery. Graham bolted ahead of her. 'Hang on a minute,' she shouted, stopping to catch her breath and noticing how the sun shone differently in this place, as if glowing through stained-glass windows. 'We're going to have a rest.'

Rita parked the pram and flipped the small brake. She checked Jimmy and her youngest, Donny, were shaded by the pram's hood. Their eyes were closed, their mouths puffing sleepy breaths, and she congratulated herself on her good timing, on only having the wide-awake Graham to keep under control, on doing something right for once. Rita pulled the bag off the wire tray under the pram and dug out a bottle of pop. She sat on a low wall, waving the bottle to entice Graham.

'Got a straw?' he said. He was panting and his face was flushed.

'Yes, a box full,' Rita replied. She uncapped the bottle and gave it to him.

'Jimmy's too old for this.' Graham poked the

battered Silver Cross with his foot, waiting for Rita to find the drinking straws. 'Pram's are for babies.'

'We can't afford a buggy,' said Rita, rummaging in her bag again. 'And Jimmy doesn't mind.'

'That's because he's a lazy bones.' Graham snatched the straws from Rita. He dropped a couple of red ones into his drink and stirred them around. Rita watched the syrupy liquid as it responded sluggishly. She ran a hand through her hair and wiped the sweat off her brow.

She'd given birth to Donny four months ago and, though still knackered, she'd begun to visit Greenacres as soon as she could walk without feeling the bruising in her gut, the nipping between her legs. Celia was living with Simon in his magnificent house up the road. It was a three-storey villa with latticed windows and two yellow-bricked chimneys and a front garden with a weeping-willow tree and a long curving drive. Celia had told Rita 'to come round anytime'. And Rita had been, every day almost, except she'd yet to find the courage to enter, to knock on the door even. She'd look at the house, marvelling at the change in Celia's circumstances, and the longer she looked the further the house seemed to recede, and the more she felt her distance from her friend.

'She's so lucky,' Rita had sighed to Collis.

'Why?' Collis asked. 'She's got no kids, no stability. She can't keep a man for more than a fortnight.'

'Simon's lasted longer.'

'He'll ditch her soon enough.' Collis sat in the living room with baby Donny on his chest.

Rita hovered in the doorway, one eye on Graham and Jimmy who were in the bathroom. 'Don't pee on the floor,' she shouted. 'Aim straight.'

'She's a fly-by-night,' Collis continued. 'And she won't be able to hold her own in that place.'

‘She’s not a slob, Collis,’ Rita returned. ‘Celia may be from Crossforth but she’s no slob.’

‘Let’s not get into an argument,’ Collis said.

‘But what do you expect her to do?’ Rita persisted. ‘Live in the same crap we do? Slum it like us, because that’s what she was born to? Is that what you’re saying?’

‘You’re tired, Rita. You need an early night.’

Greenacres was the oldest part of Cranley. It was solid and prosperous, rooted and integral to the town. It ran alongside the ancient wall which surrounded the ruin of Cranley Castle, and every Thursday, during Rita’s childhood, the *Cranley Gazette* had dedicated a page to it. Rita’s father had read the page aloud – the calendar of parties, business lunches, W.I. lectures, and church services; the profiles of prominent worthies; the column devoted to the Residents’ Association, their minuted deliberations over the respective merits of grass verges and black mini-railings and chunks of the whitest limestone. ‘If only I had their problems,’ Ernest would say, his voice coloured with desire and envy.

He’d call Greenacres ‘Snob Land’. Then every Saturday night, when he checked his Pools coupon, his guard would come down and he’d whisper, ‘Eight draws. Give me eight draws.’ Like a prayer, a mantra. ‘Eight draws and we’ll buy one of those lovely white houses.’

But his numbers never came up, and, ‘Subsidence,’ he’d say. ‘Snob Land is riddled with it. Those houses will collapse in thirty years, and where will the rich bastards be then? Homeless. Looking for lodgings. They could come here, what about that? Sit on our pan and freeze their nuts off.’

‘Ernest!’ Rita’s mother would say.

Rita’s first visit to Greenacres hadn’t been planned. It had been before she’d met Collis. She’d been on a girls’ night out, and had wandered there on her way home.

Her eyes had been bleary and her body busy with drink but she'd known the place immediately. There'd been a smell in the air, clean and open and safe. Rita had slowed to a stroll. She'd felt free and uncrowded: there had been no people about, and the houses had been hushed, standing yards back from the roads.

Rita had found a grassy bank on the corner of a junction and had sat down. The sky had been purple and dotted with stars, unlike the sky in Crossforth Devices. It hadn't been hemmed with lengths of roof and rows of chimneys, or blurred with a film of coal-fire smoke. It had been wide-screen, panoramic and untainted. Rita had marvelled at it, and as she'd marvelled the damp grass had soaked through her skirt and wet her backside. But she hadn't moved. She'd watched the sky and felt the damp, and she'd cried. Because it hadn't seemed right. To have all this. To want all this.

Rita shuffled her bottom on the wall, the edges sharp against her buttocks, and looked across the road, over the body of the tub-shaped pram. Opposite was a slim and sleek house with wrought-iron balconies curving round the top-floor windows. The balconies were home to flowering shrubs, recently hosed. Water, pearlised by the sun, trickled lazily off leaves and petals to pitter on the dry pebbled drive below.

'Are we going to see Auntie Celia now?' Graham asked. He blew down his straw to make his pop bubble.

'In a minute,' Rita replied.

'And Mummy?'

'Yes?' Rita pushed her bag beneath the pram.

'Are we going inside today?'

'Maybe.' Rita stood to check on Jimmy and Donny. 'But it does depend, Graham. Auntie Celia might not be in.'

'Oh.'

Rita stared at her infants in the pram. Donny made sucking motions with his mouth. Rita felt under the sheet for his dummy. 'It would be nice to talk to her though, wouldn't it?'

'Yes,' said Graham, blowing more bubbles.

Donny was Collis's favourite. He would tickle him under his chin, laugh when he laughed.

'Imagine what the next one'll be like,' he kept saying. 'They're getting better every time. Don't you think, Rita? Imagine the next one.'

'You don't have him all day,' Rita replied. 'He's not always so sweet.'

'Another baby,' Collis persisted. 'And the Council will give us a house.'

'I wouldn't bank on it, Collis.'

'Mummy?' Jimmy opened his eyes.

'Hello, darling, had a nice sleep?' That didn't last long. Jimmy's naps were getting shorter, and soon, Rita knew, he'd be pestering her constantly like Graham, pestering her towards total exhaustion, an exhaustion from which she could see no reprieve, especially not if Collis had his way.

Rita lifted Jimmy from the pram. 'Come on, darling, let's get your shoes on.'

'Hello Jimmy,' said Graham, tweaking his brother's feet. 'We're going to Auntie Celia's.'

Jimmy began to grizzle. 'You're hurting him,' said Rita. 'Let go.'

'I'm not,' said Graham. He continued to pinch and Rita nipped him hard on the arm in return. 'Ow!'

'I told you to stop it.'

'You *hurt* me! ' Graham stared at Rita and Rita stared back. His eyes were hard and angry, and Rita knew it was hopeless. There could be no visit today. She had this, her awkward troublesome children, and they had no place in Greenacres. Celia could wait. Rita sighed. She hoped Celia could wait.

Rita kick-released the brake on the pram as a woman, a Greenacres' type, dressed in scarlet trousers and chiffon top, skipped out of the house opposite. Graham started to cry, and the woman glanced across. 'Hush,' Rita said to him. 'You're showing us up.'

The woman shook her head, jumped into a black MG and reversed down the drive, out on to the road. Rita saw her clearly then – heavily made-up with Sindy-doll hair – and she wondered if the woman knew Celia, if she was friends with her. The woman blanked Rita. Her face was set as she shifted through the car's gears, as Graham bawled.

'Just stop it,' Rita snapped.

'You're a cow,' Graham sobbed.

'Right.' Rita watched the MG beetle off down the road. 'Home. Now.'

Celia

Rita is my best friend. She is my oldest friend. We go back a long way.

We're not the same as when we first met, obviously. We were girls then and now we're in our middle years. No longer as silly but still whizzing with energy, still having fun. We laugh so much. I suppose you could call us optimistic.

Rita and I don't really talk about the past because we're much more interested in Now. Our lives are brilliant these days, quite wonderful, and why should we bring ourselves down by dwelling on what's been and gone? Of course Rita has her problems with Collis, that will never go away. But who would have thought it? She is so successful. She has money. She's plumper than she should be, but overall she's kept her looks. And, like me, she's brimming with confidence.

I think our friendship survives because it is so equal, we've had similar experiences. Okay, so I haven't had kids and I've never had my own husband, especially one who got mangled in a pie factory. But I've had my ups and downs, and I've always been able to put myself in Rita's shoes. I've always understood what she's been going through, and I've tried to help out. When Rita and Collis were courting and needed some time alone together I had my brother lend them his car and this man, who was besotted with me, lent them his bed, until he caught me, French knicks down, with a red-haired butcher. And, though Rita can be a bit tight, she's tried to help me too. She gave me the idea for my business, my first contract, and she always doles out good advice when I need it.

I will admit to some jealousy. Especially when Rita bought her place in Greenacres, because I used to live there and I loved it and I still haven't managed to move back. She invites me round often and I always go to her garden parties, but I say no to anything else. She wants her master bedroom restyled and I can't bring myself to do it, because it feels like she's rubbing salt. Still, it's not worth falling out over. She's only wanting to be a proper friend to me, same as I am to her.

Actually, I can get quite weepy when I talk about her. Rita is so important to me. I've heard some people call her ruthless and cold and a bit of a bitch, and perhaps she is. But these people are outsiders. They only see Rita the businesswoman. They've never seen beyond her smart suits and efficiency.

But I've been privileged. I've seen Rita in her entirety; the big-hearted, big-feeling, big woman she is.

Pleasure and Pressure

Garsten Street's Delicatessen and Restaurant is one of Rita's favourite places. The shop is light and airy, with a marble-effect floor, whirring ceiling fans and orange-washed walls. The goods are displayed in glass-fronted cabinets which resemble bookcases. One cabinet is packed with pasta wrapped in cellophane and tagged with the delicatessen's own brown-paper labels. The pasta is various and exotic. There are pretty blue bows and dark green ribands. There are tubes which, because they are pink, make Rita think of internal organs of the womanly type. She glances at them as she passes with Bill, but she does not point them out as she once did when visiting with Celia.

'Every time I come in here I think never again,' growls Bill.

'You've no style,' Rita observes.

'I have. It's just different to this.'

Rita smiles. 'Rough.'

Bill smiles too. 'Not poncey.'

'Rough,' Rita says again as they enter the restaurant at the rear of the shop.

The restaurant has turquoise walls and a pine floor. There are two waitresses, a mother-and-daughter team, who wear their long black hair in swinging plaits, and have a Chaplinesque way of walking on their heels. The oval tables are draped with embroidered cloths. The three-legged stools have triangular tops. There is the smell of garlic and spices and the sound of a sunny guitar and happy voices coming from the kitchen, and there is a set menu which reads like a short story:

Today our chef Michael will be cooking a simple meal of two courses. There will be no starter. He is putting all his energy into the main dish which will feature porgy and sea kale. Our waitresses – Sophie and Matilda – have been gathering soft fruit of the genus Fragaria and these will form a frosted dessert sprinkled with toasted breadcrumbs and whipped cream. Michael's mother has been baking again and her biscuits may be sampled with coffee after the meal. She has chosen to diversify and today her biscuits are shaped-representations of Buckingham Palace. Any customers pining for her Leaning Tower Of Pisa ginger snaps should make a date for next Tuesday.

'A table for two,' Bill says to Matilda, the daughter-waitress, who smiles a slanted smile.

'Certainly, Mr Henley.' Matilda's lips let out the words sideyways as if she is whispering a secret. She then directs Bill and Rita to a table tucked beneath the menu board. 'Mrs Swales,' she says holding out her arm for Rita's jacket. Matilda hangs the jacket on a hook as Rita and Bill sit. 'I'll be back for your order.'

The table is small and Rita and Bill face each other and the space between them is chest-tightening.

'Well,' says Bill.

'Well,' Rita replies.

'Well.' Bill sucks in breath as if he is short of it. 'She's a nice girl, isn't she?'

'Who? Matilda?'

'Yes.' Bill sucks in more breath. 'Efficient. And Philippa. She's a nice girl too. You can trust her. She's efficient. And I'm stuck with Josie.'

'Not such a nice girl.'

'No.' Bill stares at Rita and there is something in his eyes that Rita likes, but doesn't.

'I know you only got a quick look when you passed, but what do you think of the agency?' she then asks hurriedly. 'The balloons and the flowers?'

'Good. It's looking good.'

'There's still lots to do.'

'Such as?'

'I'm waiting on the caterers.'

'You are?'

'Yes.'

There is a silence, and Rita searches for Matilda to fill it. She cannot think where the girl has got to. The menu is set. They don't need time to consider it.

'Rita?' Bill has his hand on the table.

'Those coat-hooks,' Rita suddenly says. 'My parents used to have some like that in their terrace, in the hall. Ugly things, but I suppose they're in fashion again.'

'Was this in Crossforth?' asks Bill, his hand idling, waiting.

'Yes.' And then Rita holds her tongue, knowing it wouldn't do to open up about her past, to let Bill think he's uncovering something, getting somewhere. Not when she isn't sure what it is she's offering, or wanting from him. 'Matilda!' A relieved Rita spots the waitress and waves. 'We're ready.'

Michael's Special tastes nutty and fishy and salty. It tastes subtly of semen and Rita, enjoying herself now, rolls it on her tongue, pushing it against her teeth, her gums. It reminds her of that night months and months after Collis's accident when Rita, finally, coaxingly, persuaded him to come.

'I want more,' Bill suddenly says to Rita, disturbing her reverie.

'Yes, scrumptious,' she replies.

Bill lays his cutlery on his plate, wipes his lips with his serviette. 'No, not the food,' he says, as Rita scoops another forkful of porgy.

'Pardon?'

'Please put that down.'

Rita watches Bill's big fingers search for the table's edge. They find it and grip tightly, turning the pink beneath the nails to white. Rita puts down her forkful, realising Bill is about to say something stupid. 'Don't,' she warns.

'But what is the problem?' Bill speaks in a hurried whisper. 'Is it Collis? It can't be Collis. You wouldn't be around me so much if your marriage worked. Collis is half a man. He's not there for you, Rita. He's not what you need.'

Rita grips her wine-glass. She gulps the wine and it is fresh and cold and fruity but she can't appreciate it. What is it about today? Is her moon eclipsing her sun, are her planetary aspects decidedly dodgy? If her boy Donny was to draw up her astrological chart (he has just completed a correspondence course with Successful Stargazers and is keen to practise) then would it advise Rita to avoid, in particular, all Take Five Video Store personnel on Monday 10th July 1995? 'Don't force it, Bill.'

'But you're not happy.' Bill picks up his knife and begins to tap it on his plate.

'I am very happy,' says Rita. 'And don't do that.'

Bill puts down the knife. 'I am in love with you,' he replies.

'Bill, shut up,' she says.

The rest of the meal passes in silence. Occasionally Bill glances at Rita, and Rita – feeling his eyes on her – ripples. She lusts after him. And maybe she loves him too. She does not know. She just feels sweaty with his attention, his declaration. He has complicated things and this has annoyed her. But she is excited too. One of the points of the triangular-topped stool is between her thighs. She presses herself against it as she eats her dessert, and as she bites into her strawberries Rita feels their tender juice slide downwards to mingle with her own.

More Pressure, Less Pleasure

Rita chooses six lemons. She picks them off the cardboard tray – turning them over one by one – discarding those with shrivelling skin or softening, mouldy rind. She does not want any duds.

'What are they like?' asks Bill.

'Fine,' Rita says. She places her lemons in the wire basket looped over her arm and walks to the checkout near Mr Fruity Man's exit. Bill follows and his hugeness, his doggedness, bears down on Rita. She wishes he'd go away.

'You might need some cherries as well,' he suggests.

'No,' Rita is stern. 'Lemons will do. Nothing too fancy.'

'I'll pay for them,' Bill offers.

'There's no need.'

Rita places the lemons on the conveyor belt which judders along to the till. The woman working the till is scrawny with a florid lovebite on her neck. She is dressed in a Mr Fruity Man green overall patterned with bunches of bananas, and a Mr Fruity Man hat which resembles a 'nana going into orbit. She looks foolish, and Rita almost feels sorry for her, except the woman is slow at her job and speaks sleepily and sloppily to the customers.

'Ninety-nine pence,' she says.

'Please,' Rita reminds her.

'Please,' the assistant grudgingly responds. She holds out her hand for the money and Bill beats Rita to it, leaning across to pay. The woman tips the money into the till, rips off a receipt and drops it on top of the lemons.

'Thank you,' Rita says.

'No problem,' Bill replies.

'Not you,' Rita growls.

'Oh.' And Bill sounds hurt.

But Rita cannot find it in her to console him. She's had enough. She's feeling cornered, and she wants to go back to work. Rita glares at the assistant. 'I mean Miss Manners here.'

'Thank you,' the assistant replies unfazed.

'And yes, *please*.' Rita continues to glare. 'I would like a carrier.'

The assistant casually removes one from a hook beneath the till. The bag is green and decorated with the obligatory bananas. The assistant lays it – her actions leisurely, unhurried – on to the conveyor belt, and Rita swoops it up, pulls it open and bundles her lemons into it.

'Do come again,' Rita persists.

'Do come again,' says the assistant, fingering her lovebite.

'Thank you.' Rita smiles a brittle smile. 'I will.'

A cooling breeze blows outside Mr Fruity Man's. It ruffles the emerald-green plasti-grass frill which is stapled to a trestle table. The table is pushed against the shop's display window. Boxes of fruit and ailing white cabbages lie higgledy-piggledy on top of it. They exude a smell of rot.

Rita sniffs. 'I'm going to report Mr Fruity Man.'

'Another one lowering the tone,' says Bill. He looks at Rita. The breeze and the still-hot sun and the ruffling plasti-grass mingle with her voluptuousness. 'South Sea Islands,' he thinks.

And Rita catches the thought: she sees it passing over his face, sees Bill's rugged features go mushy. She could get this man to do anything for her. She's known this for a long time, but now she realises it is more than true.

'Right, Bill.' She is officious, cool, confused. 'I must get on.'

'Wait a minute.' He leans towards her, tugging something from his jacket pocket. 'Please. Don't forget this. Your dad's tape.'

New Horizons?

Saturday. Collis was working, and Rita's mother was coming over to mind the kids so Rita could do a big shop. Rita sat at the breakfast-table writing her list. Toilet rolls. Matches. Milk. Bread. Tea bags. Baked beans. Fish fingers. Cream cleanser. Potatoes. On and on. Her cupboards were bare and the local was too expensive and too poorly-stocked to replenish them. It would have to be KwikSave which meant taking the Flying Fox into town.

Collis had been right. Rita's fourth pregnancy had entitled them to a council house, a large yellow-bricked semi plumb in the middle of Cranley Council's most successful development. Not the twin towers in Crossforth, which were already in need of their second lot of damp-proofing, but New Horizons, a mini version of a new town, a planner's model brought to life on a greenfield site at the edge of Cranley.

It had been Rita's and Collis's first choice, but it was the first choice of anyone who applied for a council house in Cranley. So Rita had opened the letter informing them of their allocation, expecting to be disappointed. She read the letter once, twice. She couldn't believe it. Three times. She screamed and dropped to the floor, on her knees, her fourth child lurching wildly in her belly, and she wept.

Grass verges, wide roads, interconnecting lanes! Some shops, a primary school, a pub! All that space! Three bedrooms! A nice outlook to the front and rear!

They moved in within the month, and Collis made Rita a plaque for the front door. She'd already decided on the name: '*Rita's Nest.* Because I think I'm going to settle here. You know, feel like I belong.'

Rita put her list and purse in her pocket, and then started mopping the kitchen floor, trying to get the house clean for her mother. 'Get out of my way!' she snapped at her eldest two. 'And calm down!'

They were sparring. Graham had found the plastic freebie in the box of Rice Krispies and was teasing Jimmy with it. 'Here it is. Here it is.' He dangled the purple monster above Jimmy's head. Jimmy jumped and grabbed for it, jumped and grabbed. His fat face was sweaty and pink, his mouth wobbly with frustration. Graham allowed him a touch, then pulled the model away. Jimmy began to cry. He fisted Graham in the stomach. Graham began to cry too.

'For Christ's sake. Shut it!' Rita shouted, her voice jolting the child inside her.

'Baby,' said Donny, who was sitting at the breakfast bar. He pointed to Rita's bulge which was rippling.

'Yes,' Rita replied. She pushed the mop under Donny's chair and he reached out and poked her. He caught her eye – 'Ow!' – and she dropped the mop.

'Hurt?' Donny asked, repeating the poke, this time jabbing her arm.

'Don't!' Rita said.

Donny's face creased, and so Rita grabbed his hands, patting them furiously, wanting to prevent him from crying too. There. There. She patted his plump and lovely hands, slowing to savour his skin, the smoothness of it, the warm podginess. Rita loved the feel of all her children and she could lose herself in it. There. But if she took all three in her arms they would struggle to escape, they couldn't stand being cooped up together. And if she took just one aside, lingered over him alone, the others would become jealous. And then the unplanned, almost furtive moments like now, were always spoilt by something or other, soured even by her own bad temper. 'Belt it!' she suddenly heard herself shout at Graham and Jimmy. 'Belt it!'

'Mummy!' Donny pulled away from her and he screeched, his cries more piercing than his brothers'.

'Boys, *please*,' Rita begged, and the baby inside kicked her guts. Christ. She clutched at the pain. Not this as well. She had four weeks of carrying left and she wanted it over and done with. This baby was as restless as the others had been; but worse, it was big. The biggest yet. A big hulking boy, who occupied her body with no shame, no consideration. No girl would dare treat her so bad.

The doorbell rang. Rita glanced at her watch. Right on time. Fuck. She straightened, tried to stand tall. 'Now!' she shouted, as the baby slid on to her bladder and shot wet into her pants. 'That's Grandma.' Rita seized her eldest two – 'Quiet!' – and she shook them silent. 'She'll not want to see us in this state, and she'll not want to see that mop. Graham, put it out the back, and Jimmy, tidy yourself and tidy Donny. I'm going to answer the door before Granny does a runner.'

Rita struggled off the Flying Fox with her shopping-bags. 'Thanks,' she said to the driver though she'd rather have kicked him. He'd bolted a red light. He'd splashed a crowd of pensioners coming from Lucky Balls Bingo Hall. And he'd taken a corner so fast a family-size pack of fish fingers had jumped from one of her carriers.

She'd tried to stamp on the box with her wellies but it had disappeared under her seat, and the smirking teenager across the aisle had caught it. 'Fish,' he'd whispered, returning the slippery item to Rita. 'Fish.'

And stupidly she'd thanked him too.

Rita placed the bags on the pavement. She watched the mini-bus zoom off, the smoke from the exhaust spiralling out, the tyres shining purply-blue as they whirled over the wet road, the teenager at the rear window now, signalling obscenely – finger and thumb forming a circle, a finger of the other hand entering the circle and retracting, in and out, in and out.

Rita's trackpants stuck damply to her calves and her anorak clung to her back. She tightened her hood and felt the rain as it fell on her bare hands. She was soaked and she was shattered, weighed down by everything she was having to carry.

'No! Not here!' a girl squealed.

Rita looked up. The girl was across the road, sheltering in the doorway of the New Horizons pub, perhaps waiting for the Fox back into town. She was in the arms of a boy who was holding her fast, his hands moving over her backside, squeezing her ample buttocks.

'Get your own life, Missus!' the boy shouted at Rita, and Rita quickly dropped her gaze, catching a glimpse of the sign, fixed into a grimy mound of concrete, outside the pub. The sign advertised Sheila Dawn. It only ever advertised Miss Dawn. The blonde-haired blue-eyed skinny-malink who sang at the pub on Wednesdays and Saturdays. She was supposed to be good and Rita wondered if she and Collis might go to hear her this evening, if Agnes would stay on and mind the kids some more. But no, Rita relied on her mother too much; Collis said so and Ernest did, too, whenever he could be bothered to speak to her. Besides, the last time she arranged a night out Collis forgot and went drinking with his mates and Agnes arrived to find her in tears. 'He's such a bastard.' Rita wept as her mother scurried about, putting away the children's toys, wiping toddler hand-prints off the doors. 'He doesn't understand. He just doesn't care.'

Rita sighed and bent to gather her goods. She distributed the loads evenly – four light in one hand, and a heavy and two light in the other – and then she straightened, feeling the carriers pull and cut into her palms, feeling the baby flip inside her. She glanced across at the couple, kissing long and slow, the girl ruffling the boy's hair, opening her eyes. The girl stared at Rita, and Rita steeled herself for more abuse. But no catcalls came, and only the sound of her Wellingtons, the soft slapping of rubber on wet paving, accompanied Rita as she struggled down the street and round the corner, as she made for the alley she had to navigate, the steep hill she had to climb.

Bright and Breezy, Lemon Squeezy

A breeze tenderly frisks Rita's calves as she steps over the agency threshold. 'I'm back,' she calls to Philippa, who sits working on the computer.

'Oh, hello, Mrs Swales,' smiles Philippa, looking up from the screen.

Rita uses her buttocks to push the door shut, and is slapped by a whoosh of closeness. Her delightful work-space has been cooking in her absence. It is chokingly muggy. Rita pulls the door open again and kicks a stop under the jam. 'That's better,' she says, walking over to Philippa, and glancing at the woman who sits on the office sofa, flicking through the agency leaflets. 'Who?' Rita asks, lowering her voice.

'Your interviewee,' Philippa whispers. 'Joanna Holland.'

'She's early.'

'I know.'

Joanna looks at Rita and smiles. 'I'll be with you in a

minute,' Rita responds, then jiggles the carrier and says to Philippa, 'I've been shopping. Lemons.'

'Did you get the video too?'

'Of course. A cops and robbers. In Portuguese.'

'Portuguese?'

'Mmm.'

The staff quarters are cooler. Rita takes off her jacket and drapes it over the coat-rack. She places the citrus fruit in the Iced Diamond, and the fridge – throbbing pleasantly – puffs bracing white air on to her hands. Her wedding band and eternity ring glitter in the fridge's phosphorescence. She straightens, and unzips her handbag.

Her bag is shaped like a briefcase, a womanly version trimmed with tassels. She rummages around its voluminous velvety interior, searching for her body-spray. She cannot find it. She removes her father's video to get a better look, and, as she does so, she recalls Bill outside the fruiterer's.

He gave her the tape, chancing then to kiss her cheek, whispering, promising, his breath smelling of porgy, 'I'll be round later.'

He'll be round later.

Rita puts the video on the sink-drainer and hurriedly returns to her bag. She locates the shiny purple canister labelled *Exotique* and she uncaps it. She squirts – ahh! – the compressed oriental whiff down her cleavage, along her legs. Good. She's feeling good now. Now she's back in her agency and about to fill her mind with nothing but housesitting business. Which, she tells herself, is all she wants.

'So, Nolene hasn't arrived yet?' Rita pauses by Philippa's desk, watching as she amends the mailing database.

'Not yet,' says Philippa, tapping the return key.

Rita sees her clients' names and addresses scroll down the screen. She smells Philippa's perfume, and her own body-spray, and the sweet freshness of the flowers decorating the office, and she takes it all in. She has come so far, and sometimes she pinches herself, amazed she has come so far and it is for real, not a dream.

'What were we talking about?' she asks Philippa, shaking her head, her wandering mind, promising herself to stop boozing at dinner-time.

'Nolene,' replies Philippa. 'I suppose I won't be able to take my lunch until she's back?'

''Fraid not.' Rita nods. 'Or hang on until I've done this interview. Then, if she's still not here, just go.'

'Thanks.' Philippa smiles. 'And, Mrs Swales,' she adds. 'I won't even mention what I'm not supposed to mention.'

Rita puts a hand on Philippa's shoulder and squeezes. It is a gentle squeeze but hard enough to warn. 'Very wise,' she agrees.

Rita strides over to her desk, locates Joanna Holland's folder and glances through it. There is a passport-sized photo clipped to the initial letter of enquiry and a word-processed curriculum vitae. Rita was impressed when she received this and she phoned Joanna immediately, arranged for her to come in.

Rita examines the photo as she walks to the sofa. Joanna has the right kind of face, bordering on plain but not unpleasant. Her hair is too short, too masculine, but she has put on her make-up nicely and she wears a delicate pair of earrings.

Joanna rises to greet Rita. She holds out her hand. 'Am I acceptable?' she asks.

She is tall, thin, and wears a purple short-sleeved blouse covered in black embossed dots and a black pencil skirt. Rather dramatic and perhaps too bohemian for

Rita's clients? Her eyeshadow is the same colour as the blouse – a nice co-ordinating touch – but she has applied it less subtly than in her photo, dragging it out from her lids to create a Cleopatra look. Definitely too bohemian. A line of sweat shines on her nose, and Rita glances at her armpits to see rings there too, and as she grips Joanna's hand – 'Rita Swales. Sorry to have kept you waiting' – she feels the suck of dampness. Much too bohemian.

The shake reminds Rita of the nasty things her boys used to do with their juvenile palms cupped together, pumping them in and out to make squelchy fart sounds. Rita breaks free, resists the urge to dry herself on her skirt.

'Coffee?' Rita asks. 'Tea?'

'Your assistant gave me a glass of water.' Joanna Holland smiles.

'Water,' confirms Rita. 'Well, that's good. Do you need a top up?'

'Please, that would be lovely.' Joanna passes her empty glass to Rita, and Rita, on the verge of handing it over to Philippa, catches the unpleasant tang of Joanna's body odour. It worms up Rita's nose, making her cough.

'Excuse me.' She coughs again. 'Shan't be a minute.'

Rita enters the toilet. She takes a gulping drink from the tap, pats her lips dry on the hand towel. She squirts a good dollop of liquid soap on to her palm and rubs and rubs and then rinses thoroughly, watching herself in the mirror. She's looking a little drawn, not as perky as earlier. She's probably ready for her oestrogen boost, a new HRT patch. She examines herself more closely, running a fingernail under her eye and snagging a tiny pocket of grey skin with her nail's tip. Horrible. She'll have to put concealer on that.

Rita swiftly disguises the grey skin, then she

rummages in her cosmetics case for a patch. She undoes her blouse, rips the old patch off her arm, putting the new one on her backside because she'll be wearing her sleeveless party dress later and does not want to reveal to the world, to the small business world in particular, that she's on medication. Because any whiff of sickness and the gossip will start and then the damage will be done. Rita knows. Rumours of ill-health are as bad as rumours of unreliability. Clients will lose confidence. Investors and suppliers will treat her warily, worrying she may peg it before their accounts – monies owed, interest promised – are settled. Her competitors will have a field day.

Rita shivers. She does up her blouse, puts the cosmetics case back under the sink and leaves the toilet. She opens the Iced Diamond, and lifts one of Nolene's bottles of mineral water, and pours it into a glass, telling herself she must focus her thoughts on the job in hand, on Ms Joanna Holland. She throws the empty bottle away, cautioning herself to judge Joanna fairly. (The woman may know she needs help on the hygiene and presentation fronts. She may welcome Rita's obvious expertise here. And she could have other qualities: a polite and gentle nature, intelligence, resilience.) Rita puts on a smile, steps round the partition with the water.

'Well!' she declares, seeing Nolene struggle into the agency with a dry-cleaning bag draped over one arm, a carrier hanging off the other. 'Who's this!'

'I'm aching all over, Mrs Swales,' Nolene complains. 'Your dress and things. They're so heavy.'

'You poor old soul,' Rita replies. 'Take them through to the back, freshen up and then relieve Philippa. She's been hard at it all morning.'

'She has?'

'She has.'

'But so have I.'

'Nolene, don't argue. We have a visitor.'

'Oh sorry.' Nolene glances at Joanna Holland. Joanna smiles, and Nolene smiles in return. 'Is that thingy Salcott?'

'Shush no, she arrives later,' Rita replies. 'Now chop, chop!' Rita watches Nolene pass by, and then she turns to Joanna. 'Your water,' she says. 'Viva Spring with a hint of coriander and a dash of lime!'

Nolene

Had enough of school. I wanted to be away from it. I wanted to get a job and get some money. I like clothes and CDs and make-up and going to the pictures and Freak, the best club, the only club in Cranley. They all cost.

My Dad said I was being daft, nobody walks from school into a job, not nowadays. And then, when I did get this job, my Dad said I wouldn't be able to hack it. He thinks I'm a numpty. He's never liked me. Maybe because I don't look much like him. I have a sticky-up nose and his is crooked and lumpy. He's ugly. He used to scare me when I was little. He'd come into my room at night and push his ugly face right up to my sleeping face and go, 'Aargh!' He's a bastard. Mum is nicer but then she's pathetic. She's always going on at me for being too fat and, because she's always going on at me, I'm always trying some stupid diet or other. Mrs Swales, my boss, thinks that's hilarious. She doesn't believe in dieting, and you can tell.

Sometimes my Dad and Mrs Swales seem like twins.

Dad's not fat but he's nasty, and Mrs Swales can be nasty. She doesn't have a big hooked nose but she bosses and shouts at me and she's always taking the piss. She's got this idea about me. She thinks I'm a 'loser in love', always winding me up about getting a man. She thinks she's an expert in that area, but you only have to look at her crip of a husband to see she's not. Besides, I don't like men. I like women. I'm out in the club but I'm not out anywhere else. I'm out to the people who count.

Mrs Swales would probably have a fit if she knew. She's very straight, and so is Philippa, the office suck-up. You know, I try my best. I'm not lazy or anything, and I want the job experience. But housesitting isn't for me. It's not reality. Who pays good money to have someone look after their house? What's wrong with neighbours? I said this to Mrs Swales once and she told me housesitting is a growth area and growth areas mean success and success isn't to be sniffed at. Which is true. Because I'd like to be successful. Definitely. Because I look at Doreen Abbs and Mrs Swales. I look at Josie, or that woman Celia and Mrs Swales, and know which one I'd rather be. But Philippa's her favourite, and, no matter what I do, Philippa always does one better in Mrs Swales's eyes. And there's no competing with that.

Clean People, Dirty People

Rita peruses Joanna's application. 'Now,' she says cagily. 'I haven't any vacancies at present. But I was very interested in your letter and thought it would be worth us having a little chat. Then, all being well, and if you're willing, I could keep your details on file. That would be for a permanent position. I also hold a list of relief sitters who I use for cover at short notice. It's possible you might suit one of these positions in the first instance. Now, your employment history and why you might want to work for the agency.' Rita scrutinises Joanna's CV. 'You do have some impressive qualifications and you were a highly paid technician for Vinvictor Rubber until, let's see, a couple of months ago. Perhaps you can tell me how you came to leave this job?'

Joanna Holland coughs. She crosses one slim leg over the other and pushes her fingers through her short hair. 'I was offered voluntary redundancy and I took it. Vinvictor Rubber Inc. is in a bad way, despite an upsurge in the market. The demand for rubber is increasing but the company is too inefficient to meet it. The infrastructure is antiquated, an unworkable edifice. Besides I had held my post for ten years and felt it was time for a change.'

'You did?' Rita takes a pen from her desk-tidy and removes its cap. She opens a notepad.

'I did.' Joanna Holland sips her water while Rita jots a few pointers. *Infrastructure!* Rita writes. *Unworkable edifice!!*

Joanna Holland swallows, then continues, unfazed by the note-taking. 'I was getting rather fed up spending my days dressed in a white overall and cloth cap. And I stank of chemicals, many of them ammonia-based. The lab was scrubbed frequently but you couldn't erase the urine smell. It seeped through everything. It got into your hair. I was having to wash it every night. That's why I had it cut in the end, to make the washing easier.'

'You are a clean person then?' Rita adds *Ammonia-based!* and *Urine!* to her notes.

'Sorry?' Joanna returns her glass to the desk.

Rita smiles. 'No offence,' she says reassuringly. 'It's just that I find there are two types of people in the world – clean people and dirty people – and I only want to employ clean people, because I know they will tidy up after themselves and not mess a client's house, they will treat everything with respect.'

'And, finally, why do you want to be a housesitter?' Rita asks Joanna.

'I want to be a housesitter,' Joanna says slowly, thoughtfully. 'Because I appreciate the value of homes. I appreciate what people invest in their homes, and I want to help them nurture their investment, help them protect it. A house is more than a place to stay. It is life. It is history. It is opportunity and ambition.'

'Very good,' Rita congratulates. She writes *10/10* on her notepad, then glances at the clock. She should speed things up; she might even close the interview here because she is almost sure Ms Holland is housesitter material. The woman is not a dafty. She may smell but she has brains. She may use long words and she may say words other people prefer to avoid but she is no weirdo. She is sensible, practical, on the ball. But no, Rita has her procedures and her procedures must be followed. She has to be 110 per cent certain of Joanna before she takes her on. Because Rita does not want another clumsy Derek or jittery Doreen. She wants wholly competent sitters who will not mither her or cut into her precious time.

So, scenarios. Rita sits straight, with her bosoms erect, and smiles. She rubs her powerful hands together, performs a one potato two potato. Psychology. Testing the interviewee. Trying to unnerve. But Joanna only watches. Patiently. Drinking from her glass.

'Scenarios,' says Rita.

'Scenarios,' repeats Joanna.

'I present a situation and you have to tell me how you think you'd respond. Okay?'

'Okay.'

A warm gust of wind blows a crisp packet through the open agency door. It distracts Rita and it distracts Nolene, who sits at Philippa's desk, sticking stamps on to letters. Nolene leaves her seat. She is now more suitably attired in a sun dress which has swirls of rainbow colour falling from under the bust to the hem. It's tight but it flatters Nolene's bigness. Nolene drops the crisp packet into the bin by Rita's desk and she smiles first at Rita, then at Joanna. 'That's what I like,' Rita says to Joanna. 'Tidy habits. Now. Are you ready?'

'I am,' Joanna replies.

One. It's 6.45 a.m., your Mini's just broken down, and you are scheduled to be at a client's house, to start a sit in half an hour's time. What do you do?

Swear, and bang my head on the dashboard.

And then?

Look out a bus timetable.

And if there's no bus?

Phone for a taxi.

Would you contact me, or the agency?

No, I would regard it as my problem, not yours.

Fine.

Two. You are partial to kebabs. You take some into the client's living room to eat and you trip over his cat and they land on the sofa, staining and skewering it. What do you do?

I can't imagine myself behaving so stupidly. Food belongs in the kitchen.

I agree, but what would your response be if you did damage a client's sofa? Would you contact the agency?

Yes, I'd phone immediately. I'd apologise and then offer to right the damage myself.

Have you the expertise?

I can eradicate stains using my grandmother's stain-buster recipe. It's made from natural ingredients and banishes the most obstinate marks (tar, ketchup, blood, semen, even soy sauce). My brother-in-law is a reputable upholsterer.

Good.

Three. A client has a restraining order out on his ex-wife. She is forbidden to step on his land. You are sitting his house and see her walking up the garden path. What do you do?

Phone the police immediately. They will deal with it.

Excellent.

Philippa returns from lunch. 'Phew,' she declares, fanning her hand round her face. 'It's still hot out there.'

'Hole in the wotsit,' suggests Nolene. 'Greenhouse thingy.'

Rita looks up. 'Less chatter, girls,' she says, glimpsing the agency clock. Goodness. Only three more hours till the party. She'd better get to grips.

Now finally, quickly, these are not scenarios, but questions I want you to answer off the top of your head. No hesitating. No pondering. Snap. Snap. Snap.

Like the Rorschach Test but without the ink-blots?

Ahem. Probably. Yes, there are no ink-blots. Now. What three words come into your mind when you think about sitting another person's home?

Responsibility. Enjoyable. Interesting.

What three words describe home to you?

Cranley. England. Mortgage.

List three things which you think make a home.

Love. Money. Time.

Rita pulls open the top drawer of her desk and removes a plastic wallet which is filled with brightly coloured paper. She walks round the desk. 'Thank you for coming,' she says to Joanna, shaking hands with her, and then proferring the wallet. 'I'll phone you tomorrow to have a chat. I must say I've been very impressed and feel you could make an excellent sitter. But of course I'll have to check your references, and you may want to think further about what we'll be asking of you. It may help if you read more about the agency. Get a proper feel for the business. Here are a few of our leaflets, which I believe you haven't seen, and also an article about Rita's Housesitting Service which was in last year's *Domicile*, the spring issue. An excellent piece. Shame they shan't be covering our anniversary celebrations.' Rita opens her arms and indicates the balloons on the partition, the streamers on the office ceiling. 'We're having a party after closing.'

'Your assistant told me,' Joanna says. 'It looks wonderful.'

'Doesn't it?' Rita replies, watching Nolene approach, carrying her purse, striding purposefully. Rita knows what this is about. Nolene wants *her* lunch *now*.

'Are you expecting a crowd?' asks Joanna.

'Yes. I was planning a small affair but it's spiralling somewhat—'

'Excuse me.' Nolene brushes past Joanna to stand beside her boss.

'Friends, business associates, the press—' Rita continues, ignoring her.

'Even me,' Nolene interjects, smiling at Joanna. 'The office stamp-licker.' Her smile is open, inviting, not her usual cheeky number or begrudging, insolent grimace. 'You should come along,' she invites.

Rita glares at Nolene. 'Well, of course,' she then says, because what else can she say? 'You'd be welcome, Ms Holland.'

'Thank you.' Joanna looks from Rita to Nolene, her Cleopatra eyes settling on the girl. 'Perhaps I will.'

Mrs Ethel Cram

I didn't recognise her at first. I was at the doctor's, woman's trouble, a dodgy womb, and I was waiting my turn, flicking through *Domicile*, a glossy number about houses, mortgages, insurance, stuff like that. Not my thing. But there was this photo of a busty woman and something about her, something in her eyes made me stop, look her over, remember. The fiery eyes of little Miss Myhill. Except she's a Mrs now, respectable, hitched to that boy Swales. Now, I never thought that would last.

Little Rita Myhill.

She was a bright bit and had a nice way about her (unlike her parents, Eff Off Ernest and Suffering Agnes) but, even with those eyes, I never thought she would amount to much. She was like a lot of girls from Crossforth. She was sex mad, and got her fair share, and the one she ended up with was, well... I wouldn't have turned him down. But he was a prude. He didn't approve of me. I thought he would sap Rita Myhill if she stayed with him for too long. Obviously that's not happened.

I don't live in Crossforth now, not even in Cranley. I got fed up with that world, surrounded by people who think they're better than you. It restricted me. There was too much gossip. I was the scrubber who'd shagged her way up. People resented me. I was never given any credit. Yet I was the one who turned the Coach and Horses around. It was bloody hard work. I loved it, but it was bloody hard work. It wore me out.

In the end I jacked it all in for a long-distance lorry driver who promised me the earth and a free trip to Paris. And that's where I lived for a time. Would you believe it? And now I'm back in Angleterre, on the east coast, shacked up with a crab fisherman. He's okay and we have a great time when the crabs come in.

I used to stand outside the door of room 48B sometimes, when business was quiet, and I'd hear little Miss Myhill. She had a mouth on her. She grunted and screamed, no shame. She wasn't backwards in coming.

And now she's married and a business woman. I was a business woman once. I was married once. Funny that.

Clean, not Dirty

Rita squirted pine-fresh cream cleanser around the toilet bowl. She squeezed the livid-green plastic container and the pungent liquid ejaculated on to the white ceramic. Then she was off smearing it round the bowl with her long-handled toilet brush, working it in, scrubbing until the excretory traces were gone. Shazaam! Disappeared into the scoop of water at the bottom of the pan.

Rita shook the brush free of suds and flushed the toilet. The water swirled and whooshed away the grime. Then, as an extra precautionary measure, she finished off the job with a capful of disinfectant thrown haphazardly under the bowl's rim. She returned the brush to its swan-shaped holder and plonked her backside on the edge of the bath. It was Friday. She always cleaned the bathroom on Friday. And then she recleaned it on the Monday after a weekend of use by Collis and the kids. Rita sighed.

'I'm home!' Collis's voice echoed downstairs in the hall.

Rita pushed her hair from her eyes – he's home – then she stood up, carefully avoiding the mirror which fronted the pine cabinet, because she didn't want to see her reflection, because she knew, could sense the way her features were shrivelling to fit her life, her face becoming as worn and perished as her mother's rubber housework mat. Rita made for the stairs.

'Hello,' Collis said, watching her descend. 'Had a good morning?'

'Nothing exciting,' she said.

'Ah, never mind.' Collis put an arm around Rita and steered her into the living room. He sat on the easy chair and patted it, and she obediently squashed next to him. Collis put a hand on her thigh. Rita felt its sticky warmth through her trousers and, staring down at it, she saw the oil staining Collis's knuckles, the dry patch caused by the sterilising chemicals he used at the factory.

Collis had changed job three times during their marriage. Originally he'd laminated kitchen units and tables, then he'd assembled furniture made from moulded plastic, then he'd chased stock for a builder's merchant, and now he maintained the packing machines and conveyor belts for Peter's Perfect Pies. At first Rita had known everything about his work, and she'd sympathised when a day had gone badly. She'd encouraged him to apply for other jobs, go for promotion, take nightclasses. But then the kids had come along and her attention had been divided, in two, then three, then four, then five. The kids and Collis. She was lost to them. She was lost to herself. And now she took Collis's wage packet but had no idea what he felt about his work. She did not know if he loved or loathed it. She did not know if he was happy at Peter's Perfect Pies, if he was being treated fairly, if he wanted out. She did not know whether a semi-skilled labourer was what Collis wanted to continue to be.

'Would you like a sandwich?' she asked.

Collis squeezed Rita's flesh with his chunky fingers.

‘You’re looking good,’ he said.

‘I’m just in my scruff.’ Rita sighed.

‘Still…’

Collis finished work early on a Friday; the boys were at school; and Rita hated the routineness of it all. ‘There’s some crab paste,’ she said. ‘And I could slice a tomato.’

‘I adore you,’ Collis replied.

Rita pulled on her underwear and then her trousers and top. Collis lay on their bed. ‘That was nice.’ He yawned.

Rita looked at her husband. Recently Collis had begun to use that tiny, sad nothing of a word. Nice. What did it mean? Rita knew what it didn’t mean. It didn’t mean wonderful or fiery. It didn’t mean what they’d had in the old days when Rita used to come like a rocket. Nice was the opposite of that. Nice was the bleak full-stop. The rocket falling dead to the earth. Nice wasn’t what Rita had been made for.

Rita straightened her clothes and fluffed her hair with her fingers. ‘I’m going for a walk,’ she said.

Collis rolled on his side and dangled an arm for his underpants. ‘I’ll come with you.’

‘No,’ Rita resisted. ‘I’ll be going to the Primary after to pick up Donny and Ben. So you’ll need to stay in for Jimmy.’

‘Graham’s got a key.’

‘Graham’s got football practice. Someone has to be in for Jimmy.’

‘And tea?’ Collis stood with his back to Rita, and pulled his pants over his buttocks. He slid his hand into the Y-front pouch and arranged himself neatly. His actions were fluid – he was still beautiful.

‘It’s all sorted. Don’t you worry.’

Afternoon

Rita takes the party check-list from Nolene. 'Thank you,' she says.

'Can I go for my lunch now?' Nolene asks, attempting to sound and look contrite.

'Manners.' Rita glances through the check-list.

'Sorry,' Nolene replies. '*Please* can I go for my lunch now?'

'That's better.'

The check-list is a computer printout divided in two: to the left the names and phone numbers of the guests, to the right the names and numbers of the suppliers and press. Rita has had Nolene ringing every guest to confirm their attendance; a little punishment for her rash behaviour earlier. The list is covered in ticks. 'So, most of them are coming,' Rita remarks.

'Yes.'

'We've got our work cut out then. Go and get your lunch while you can.'

'Yes, Mrs Swales. And *thank you*.'

Rita picks up the phone and dials Speed U's, watching Nolene, in her rainbow-swirled frock, her purse clasped in hand, disappear from the agency. 'That girl,' she says.

'She can be silly,' Philippa agrees.

'More than that,' Rita replies, as the line to the taxi firm rings out.

It rings, but no one answers. Rita waits, tapping a pencil on the check-list. 'Somebody else not doing their job properly,' she comments. She waits. She taps. 'Come on.' She looks at the check-list. She slams the receiver down. 'I can't mess about.' She picks up the receiver again – 'He'll just have to sort it' – and she presses the key pad, trying Collis.

Bring! Like Speed U's he isn't engaged. Bring! Bring! Like Speed U's there's no answer. Rita scrawls on her check-list, drawing circles around *Jenny Salcott, Cranley Gazette 724 4272*. Where is the man?

Rita then glances up, sees Bill in the agency doorway. His shirt sleeves are rolled past his elbows and his thick arms are raised, his hands clutching the doorframe. He smiles. 'Can I come in?' he mouths.

The phone continues to pipe. Rita feels a lurching in her stomach as she points to the receiver. 'Sorry,' she mouths back. 'Not now.'

Bill shrugs his shoulders – 'Okay. Later' – and he takes his hands from the frame and he leaves and an elderly woman with a shopping trolley passes, filling the doorway, his space, so completely that Rita wonders whether she imagined him. She slams the receiver down.

'So, Rita, it will be a fairly substantial piece, which is why I need to come and see you to quiz you about a few things, about your background, how you started out, why you chose housesitting etc. I would hate to get my facts wrong, to queer my reputation for accurate, honest reporting. I presume you've no objections?'

‘It shouldn’t be a problem,’ Rita tells Salcott. ‘But, let me go over this, you won’t be at the party?’

‘No.’

‘But the photographer will? Because I’d prefer the photographer to be about then.’

‘Yes, well, Rita, it wouldn’t make much sense otherwise would it?’

‘No.’

Salcott is married to a builder who advertises heavily in the *Gazette*, and she lives with him in Greenacres, has done for years. She was resident when Celia was shacked up with Simon there, and Celia can well remember her: ridiculously dressed, her hair coiffured and set hard with lacquer, beetling about in her black MG, showing up at every Greenacres’ bash to rub noses with Cranley’s finest.

A well-connected woman; the reason, Rita believes, for her position as the *Gazette*’s social-events’ reporter, by-lined and much-photographed. Though Salcott claims otherwise. ‘We are twins of experience, you and I,’ she tells Rita, recounting how she drudged as a dinner-lady by day and studied for her press qualifications by night. ‘Self-made women!’

‘Bollocks,’ Rita wants to reply, though she never does, finding herself – in order to guarantee that ‘special’ mention in ‘Salcott’s Scene’ – having to fawn instead.

‘So?’ Jenny Salcott stretches the little word out. ‘What did you think about my piece on the WOSB event?’

‘Oh tremendous,’ Rita offers.

‘Wasn’t it?’ says Salcott. ‘But those ladies do such marvellous work, and they do it so stylishly, it’s such a pleasure to write about them.’

‘Yes.’ Rita smiles. She attended the Fund-Raiser for Orphans of the Conflict In Former Yugoslavia with Celia. They went for their respective businesses, to be seen, to make and renew contacts, but not for fun, because they knew from past gatherings that the tightarsed Wives Of Successful Businessmen couldn't party on down.

The wives wore their designer frocks, and Salcott mingled amongst them, with her notepad and mini tape-recorder, decked in her usual scarlet, her hair a black synthetic-looking bob. With her wide jaw-line, wide forehead, and waxy complexion, Jenny Salcott is known as Jenny 90 and – Rita's favourite – Captain Salcott. But nobody who is anybody, who knows the value of appearing in 'Salcott's Scene', would dare use such names within her earshot.

'Such an excellent idea to serve an orphan's supper, so inventive.'

'Oh yes.' Rita and Celia had found it difficult not to convulse over the battered tin mugs half-filled with Evian and the newspaper cones barely bulging with neat triangles of wholemeal and sesame seed bread and mini slivers of oak-smoked cheese. But it got too much when the £25 a strip of five raffle not only yielded the standard prizes of health farm vouchers and dinners-for-two at Wilson's, but also 'symbolic' booby gifts: an army surplus billy-can, a china dove of peace, a child's drawing of 'playing soldiers', a candle of remembrance.

'Wonderful to see so many husbands too, supporting such a good cause. Marvellous copy.' Salcott takes a long breath. 'I can't recall your better half, Rita—'

'No,' Rita says. 'The venue was upstairs.' She criss-crosses Salcott's name out with her pencil.

'Ah, and your poor man is unable to mount, of course.'

'He will be coming today.' Rita scribbles *If the bastard turns up* on the guest list.

'Oh splendid. That will make a nice picture. Because he's such a handsome man, and it's so poignant too, seeing how he is. Wonderful copy.'

'If you say so,' Rita says. 'Until later then?' she says.

Bloody Salcott. Rita takes a pile of work from her in-tray, and she throws it into Philippa's.

'Oh!' Philippa flinches. 'What?'

'I'm delegating,' Rita snaps. 'My privilege.'

'Oh,' Philippa says. 'But—'

'No buts,' orders Rita, phoning Speed U Taxis again. They're engaged. She bangs down the receiver, then takes it up, furiously pressing the numbers for home.

'Hello.'

'Ben? Why aren't you at school?'

'Free period.' Rita's fourth and youngest child makes a clicky noise with his mouth. He's chewing gum, and Rita can imagine him. His body slumped against the hall wall. An unhappy lad.

'I see.' Which is as far as Rita is prepared to take it. 'Well, where's your dad? I want to speak to him.'

'He's in the garden.' The gum obstructs, then elongates Ben's reply. 'He's lying on his mat, yanking weeds.'

'Right. Well, do you think you can tell him I haven't been able to arrange a taxi for tonight? Speed U's constantly engaged. So it's probably best if he sorts it. I'm too busy.'

'Surprise,' Ben says.

'Pardon?'

'Pardon?' Ben mimics Rita's voice, and she knows she ought to cut the call but she can't.

'Ben, I'm not in the mood.'

Ben laughs.

'You're too old for this.'

'For what?'

Ben gobs the gum, and Rita hears the chewed blob hitting the telephone mouthpiece, and then nothing.

'Ben!' she shouts. 'Do I need this?!'

Do I?

Other Afternoons

Rita thought it might have started when Agnes fell ill and couldn't help out any more with the kids. But it was difficult to chart. It might've been bubbling under for much longer, a low unwatched and unchecked simmering which suddenly now, its timing inexplicable, was on the boil.

Erupting.

'What's going on?' Collis asked.

Rita ignored him. She yanked and scraped the chairs across the floor. She slammed them round the dining table. She glowered at the kids as they scrambled to sit. She walloped down the salt and pepper pots, cutlery and crockery.

Donny and Ben started to grizzle, and Rita thwacked them with the oven gloves. 'Shut it!' She dished up lumpy mashed potato and burnt chops, and the chops rattled as they hit the plates.

'Rita!' Collis shouted. 'Answer me!'

But she had gone to the kitchen for a saucepan. It

contained hot gravy. 'Nothing's going on,' she snapped, moving round the table now, pouring the steamy sauce over the food, dribbling it from plate to plate. The sauce was thick and charcoal-coloured. Rita spied a stray, unwanted knob of browning. She scooped it from the pan and poked at it with a fingernail, tutting noisily.

'Boys,' Collis ordered. 'Up the stairs. Now!'

'No, they don't. Tea is served!' Rita blocked the exit. She clutched the saucepan, wielding it like a weapon, ready to defend, ready to attack. Her face was greasy and red from cooking. Her hair – made shapeless by the heat – hung stringily about her shoulders.

'Rita,' Collis said, watching his wife, his voice barely steady. 'I want the kids upstairs. They shouldn't see you like this.'

'Why shouldn't they see me like this?' Rita shouted. 'This is me. This is real. I'm fed up. I've had enough. I'm fucking up to here with it all.' Rita waved a hand near her head. She kept on waving it. She couldn't stop waving it. And it was frightening.

She was breaking up, spiralling off, taking a hike to Nutsville. Rita fell back against the door. She dropped the saucepan, stopped her waving, and shivered. Then she began to cry.

Tears.

Rita switched on the television, then stood at her ironing board. Behind her on the sofa was a mound of newly washed and dried clothes. She reached for a T-shirt and laid it on the board. She spat at the iron – it hardly spluttered – and jabbed it over the creased, unresponsive cloth. She half looked at the TV and half at her chore. Her boys were at school, Collis at work. On the screen was Prime Minister Thatcher. Rita's house was empty except for herself and the family budgerigar.

The bird was caged in a bamboo dome which hung

from the living-room ceiling. It was an ugly bird, constantly on the moult; its belly and pate were patched with bald, its few feathers sparsely spread; its sheddings flitted endlessly, clouding its home. It was squawking, and Rita shouted at it.

'Shut it! I can't hear the fucking programme.'

The bird took no notice. Its tune for the day was like a fork circling on thin porcelain, and Rita wondered if one of the boys had put something in its water, if this was the bird's excruciating swan-song. 'Go on,' she thought. 'Get it over and done with.' But there was no last screech. 'Go on,' Rita willed. No dying Dicky dropping from his perch. Rita tugged a black skirt from the pile of washing and, exasperated – 'You're a waste of space!' – threw it over the cage. Dicky twittered in surprise and then fell silent. Time for bed.

Rita wished she could conk out so easily. Her limbs felt weighted and ready for sleep, and yet she was agitated, her mind fizzing. She switched off the iron and slumped in the easy chair. She'd had enough.

'Now listen,' said the television.

Rita ran her hands under the chair's cushion, searching for a tissue. She was going to blub. Again. She found one of Ben's cotton squares. It was patterned with Rupert Bear and greeny flakes of snot. Oh my God. Rita began to sniffle. She clutched the arms of the easy chair and lifted her head. Out it comes. Rita howled. Out it all comes.

'Now listen.' She heard.

Ravelling. Unravelling.

Rita spat on her mascara block. She took a tiny brush and rubbed it through the spit. She rubbed it backwards and forwards until the tablet beneath bubbled and melted to a thick black paste. She looked at herself in the mirror and blinked. She'd been avoiding this for too long.

Ben came into the bathroom. He undid his trousers, pulled down his pants, and gingerly positioned himself on the toilet. He stared at Rita. 'What you doing?'

Rita moved from the mirror. 'What do you think?' she asked, crouching in front of her son, showing him the mascara block. 'I was going to put some on.'

Ben wriggled on his seat and Rita heard something soft drop into the toilet bowl. 'Where?' he said.

'On my lashes,' Rita replied.

Ben looked uncomfortable. He fussed with the hem of his top, picked at the stitching. He needed space, and Rita obliged. 'It's almost an antique,' she said, lying the tiny brush on the block and closing its lid. She leant against the cold radiator. Then hugged her flimsy housecoat to her body. 'Like me.'

'Finished.' Ben wiped his behind and slid off the toilet seat, then pulled the flush and yanked up his trousers. 'You never get dressed now, Mummy,' he said at the door. 'And you're always crying.'

Rita tried to ruffle her son's hair. The boy pulled away and escaped to the landing. Rita called after him, 'We all get sad sometimes.'

Ben turned to face Rita. 'But I'm fed up with it,' he braved. 'We've been sad and misery—'

'Miserable,' Rita corrected him.

'Miserable for ages. It's—' Ben paused. 'Crap.'

'Ben!'

'Fucking crap!'

'Ben?'

Rita watched as her youngest stamped and stamped his feet. 'Fucking fucking crap!' His trousers loosened and slid from his backside, exposing his pants, his skinny thighs. And then his ankles seemed to go – snap – like wintered twigs – snap – and then there he was, heaped on the carpet, his body crumpled and heaving with terrible boyish sobs.

Afternoon Still

Rita opens the large filing-cabinet. She's still rattled after her calls, and needs to do some basic admin to calm herself down.

She removes a stack of head-and-shoulder shots, sits at her desk and examines each one. Her housesitters, forty of them, all photographed by Bobby Cross: a freelance expert in soft-focus, in coaxing smiles from the shy, the tense, the retiring. Bobby snaps the female housesitters against a pearly pink background and the male against a cool blue. He knows what Rita wants: gentle portraits, calming to the eye, portraits hued with decency and integrity.

Rita puts a couple to the side for archiving – Fred Barker and Cynthia Jordan, an adaptable, pragmatic pair, who had left the agency to get married and live self-sufficiently in Wales – and Philippa comes over, standing by Rita's desk, sending a shadow across Rita's arms. 'Can I give some of that work to Nolene, Mrs Swales?' she asks, gloomily, wearily. 'Only I've got so much on.'

'Fine,' Rita replies, briskly sorting.

Philippa watches her. 'Oh,' she then says. 'You're doing the profiles. Thank you.'

'Yes,' Rita replies. 'I'm not all bad.'

'Oh no, you're not, thank you.' Philippa is beaming now. 'Would you like a cup of tea?' she offers.

'That would be nice.'

Rita puts aside one more photograph for archiving (Reggie Black who was caught with his fingers in a client's jewellery box and subsequently sacked), and she puts a few in her in-tray for reprinting. Chris Bonham. Dorothy Clark. Elizabeth Scully. John Whittaker.

John was the first sitter Rita took on. The very first. An ex-schoolmaster with a quiet but commanding presence. His face is lean, his gaze steady, his white moustache and beard neatly trimmed. Rita was sure about him the moment he walked into her agency, enquiring about the card she'd put in the window: DO YOU APPRECIATE THE FINER THINGS IN LIFE? ARE YOU FLEXIBLE, CLEAN, AND STABLE, WITH AN INTEREST IN HOME SECURITY? QUALITY HOUSESITTERS WANTED. SEE MRS SWALES WITHIN.

The agency had been open for a month before that card had gone up. Rita hadn't wanted to interview for staff until she'd managed to get at least one client on her books. It had been a nerve-wracking time. A month of frenetic activity, of placing adverts and posting fliers: AFRAID TO LEAVE YOUR HOUSE EMPTY? LET US LOOK AFTER YOUR PROPERTY. RITA'S HOUSESITTING SERVICE WILL PROTECT YOUR HOME FROM SOCIETY'S UNDESIRABLES. A month of panic, of fear that the enterprise would never get off the ground, that Rita would have to jack it all in and hole up indoors again with Collis and the boys.

And she hadn't wanted that, because although they'd moved to Greenacres and were living in the roomiest, nicest place ever, the agency felt more like home to her.

It was where she truly belonged. It was the real 'Rita's Nest', her undoubted 'New Horizons'. It gave her such a thrill.

Her own business.

She tingled when she touched its furnishings, which she did often, running her hands over the filing-cabinets, the pine table, the lime-green sofa. She couldn't bear to be parted from it. She stayed late, working on its computer, experimenting with the databases she'd been learning about at night-school. And Collis complained of loneliness, and the boys of being abandoned. 'This is no good,' Collis pressurised. 'We hardly see you and we're losing money. What's the point, Rita? Cut your losses. Swallow your pride.'

But then she signed up Ron and Glenda Martin from across the road. They were planning to stay in the States for six months. They didn't want to rent out their home for that time. They wanted somebody respectable to look after it, to mow the lawn, to Hoover the carpets, to keep it warm and happy till their return. Rita will never forget them – Ron and Glenda Martin – because their custom launched her into the rough-and-tumble of transactions, competition, potential profit. When she banked their deposit she felt that, finally, definitely, Rita's Housesitting Service was on its way.

Rita sorts her last photograph, then she's back at the filing-cabinet pulling out the sitter records. 'A' for Abbs. Doreen Abbs. She took on Dithery Doreen not long after John Whittaker because she had another client by then, a widower in Greenacres. Doreen was sent by the Job Centre (Rita had given them a card too) and she was terrible to interview but she touched something in Rita which she rarely touches now. She moved her.

Rita gave John the six-month job and she gave Doreen the weekend house-and-dogsit for the widower. Doreen was so grateful. She didn't complain, not even when she had to wait an age for her next assignment, again a weekend for the widower. She seemed to accept the work would come in dribs and drabs, and this made Rita's life a little easier as she struggled to attract more clients. 'Cut your losses,' Collis persisted. 'Cut your losses.'

Rita checks Doreen's details. Her workload has increased since. Substantially so. Thank God. Things eventually improved. Very few weekend sits now, more weekly and fortnightly. The details need an update, and Rita, from memory, adds *From July 1994 to June 1995 Doreen sat for eighteen clients.* She pencils an asterix by her words and writes *Philippa cross-reference with database.*

Rita then glances over Doreen's personal statement – not in fact written by Doreen, none of the statements are in truth personal, but composed by Philippa who joined the agency in '92 to work on this and other office tasks. The statements are deliberately upbeat and open-armed. Doreen's reads: *Housesitting has given me so much pleasure. I enjoy looking after other people's homes. I care for them like I care for my own. I have been with Rita's Housesitting Service since it started, and have many satisfied clients who now ask for me personally. I hope you will become one of them.*

Rita can remember Doreen quaking as she looked this over.

'Oh dear,' she said.

'Oh dear what?' Rita asked. 'Would you prefer *I'm a shy, quiet, humble little mouse. I like housesitting because it lets me hide away*? Besides, you are very popular, Doreen.'

'Mmm.' Doreen examined the statement again. She brushed her hands over the draft, backwards, forwards, palms then knuckles. 'I don't want people getting the wrong impression,' she said.

'They won't,' Rita assured.

'I really appreciate this,' Philippa says, as she removes

the empty mug from Rita's desk.

'I know,' mumbles Rita, continuing with her work, not wanting to break her flow, to disrupt the rhythm: pick up a record with the right hand, scan it and transfer it to the left, place on one of three piles – no amendments, simple amendments, amendments to be checked against database.

'It's such a big piece of work,' Philippa persists.

Rita nods.

'But not complicated. I mean, it's just very detailed, and really, Mrs Swales, I think it eats far too much into your own time. You shouldn't have to do it. You should—'

'Let her do it,' Nolene suggests. The girl is back from her break and she leans – her lively flesh pushing against the constraining fabric of her dress – over the computer printer. She fills the printer with paper, then closes its lid. It whirs hummingly.

'Quite,' Philippa says. 'Let me do it.'

Rita stares at the card in her hand. What pile was she was going to place it on?

'Busy! Busy! Busy! That's what I like to see!' Jenny Salcott strides into the agency. 'My, isn't this nice? All these flowers, the decorations! How lovely.'

Bugger. Rita looks up to see Salcott, arms open wide, approaching fast. 'Okay.' Rita taps Philippa with the card. 'You can try. '

'Oh, gosh, thank you, Mrs Swales,' Philippa enthuses. 'Thank you. Thank you.'

'Don't gush now,' says Rita, rising from her chair, quickly straightening her skirt, smoothing out the creases with her broad hands. She nips the shoulders of her blouse between her fingertips and pulls them into line. 'Jenny! So good of you to come.' Rita air-kisses the journalist, once, twice, catching a whiff of pan-stick and hair spray.

'Rita,' says Salcott, grabbing Rita's hands, staring

into her face. 'You amaze me. You look only the tiniest bit frazzled in this heat. How do you manage it? No, it's okay, I know the answer.' Salcott releases Rita. 'Years of practice.' She rummages in her shoulder bag. 'Now, where's it got to?'

Rita watches Salcott's bowed head, her hair draping blackly, shimmering synthetically, and she reminds herself not to flinch or smile or regard Salcott's appearance in any way suggestive of disapproval or amusement. It is difficult, especially today, because, along with her femme fatale bob, Captain Salcott is sporting a red rhinestone jacket, hung with black fringing, and red plastic gaucho-styled pants which are tucked into white cowboy boots.

'Ah,' says Salcott. She pulls her mini tape-recorder from her bag, and waves it at Rita. 'Shall we?' She sprawls herself on the sofa, the silver spurs on the heels of her boots catching and twinkling with the summer light. 'Now, where shall we start?' she asks.

Ernest

She's my daughter. My only child. We tried for more, the wife and me. I wanted a lad. I get on better with lads. But it wasn't to be. And perhaps a good job too, because the one girl has been hard enough work. We had these ideas. We thought bringing up a kid was about teaching them right from wrong, letting them know they'd be punished if they did wrong, but it didn't turn out like that. We were strict with Rita but still she went off the rails. She was wilful, stubborn, bloody-minded. She still is. Rita can't be told.

And living in Crossforth didn't help. It smelt like a bog. It got inside you. It made you feel dirty, useless, like scum. Agnes did her best. She was always cleaning the house, always washing Rita. But that kind of grime can't be got rid of. It's the kind that sticks.

I think that's why Rita went the way she did. We tried our damnedest, but Crossforth was against us, and Rita turned out no different than all the others in that area, more interested in putting it about than getting on in the world.

She believed she was *it* though, and looked down her nose at her mother and me. I never thought she'd amount to much, and it came as no surprise to me when she got banged up by that boy, Swales, and married him. Well, that's the end of her, I said to Agnes, signed and sealed. No surprise.

Rita had one kid after another, and with each kid she lost the only thing she'd ever had going for her. Her looks. They went to pot, and I wanted to have nothing to do with her. But still she kept coming round. She couldn't wait to get away and no sooner did than she was back, pestering us, asking Agnes to baby-sit, knowing Agnes couldn't refuse. My wife loved those boys and Rita took advantage. Agnes wasn't happy about it, she cursed Rita, but never to her face. My wife had standards. She was proper.

But then, thank Christ, Swales had his accident, and that's when things changed. Rita had to take a long hard look at herself. And we're all benefiting now. Agnes missed out. But the rest of us ...

Well, I'm free of Crossforth and living in a decent place, and Rita's got her big bungalow and her business. I don't understand what she does. But she comes to visit me in her fancy suits. She's quite regular about that. Brings me videos; some good, most bad. My friends in the home watch out for her. They say she's a corker, and, when they whistle her, I do feel something then, proud. Rita dresses like a winner now. She does.

Questions and Answers

How did you receive the news?

I answered the door. The manager of Peter's Perfect Pies was standing on the doorstep. His face was as grey as a headstone. He was obviously a worried man: he was worried how much the accident would cost his firm. He was right to worry.

And your reaction?

Blank.

Can you describe the injuries?

He lost most of his left leg. The packing machine cut into it and it couldn't be saved. The surgeon had to amputate mid-thigh, and he made a mess. The skin around the point of amputation has been gathered and twisted like you would twist the end of a Christmas cracker or a sausage. It's stamped with uneven lines and tiny pricks where the cat-gut was threaded in and out, and it's a screaming purple even now. And I am still, after all these years, getting used to it.

And his hand?

Not as bad. It's healed better. It's pleasanter to look at. It resembles a potato or a rodent curled up. Collis used to draw eyes and a nose on it and tease the boys with it when they were younger. They found it funny.

What did you think when you saw Collis for the first time after the accident?

He's asleep, thank God.

And when you saw his injuries?

Sick. I felt sick. I felt like I'd lost a leg and fingers too. Because they had been mine. Collis's limbs had been my limbs too. Our early years together had been nothing but that. His limbs. My limbs. My limbs. His limbs.

And how do his injuries affect you now?

They disappoint me, make me feel cheated. Because I am burning now. I am vital. And I want Collis to be the same. I want him to be able to chase me, to floor me, to hold me locked between his legs. I want him to squeeze me between two whole legs, to knock the wind out of me, to make me gasp and beg.

Your sex life has been ruined?

It had gone stale before the accident. The kids, Collis's work, my depression had worn us down, tired us out. We were fed-up with each other. Collis's injuries actually brought us closer together. For a time. He was needy when he came out of hospital. He was impotent but he wanted to be touched. There was plenty of fondling. It was very intense. Then we had to experiment with positions. But now Collis cannot kiss me without crying. So now it's not so good.

You lost a lot. What did you gain by the accident?

A new me, and plenty of mail. There were letters

arriving with every post, from Peter's Perfect Pies, from Mr Ferguson our lawyer, from well-wishers.

I also discovered a talent for filing. I was storing the letters in a shoe box but it filled quickly and I was about to start another when Ferguson's receptionist said, 'Mrs Swales, think system, not box.' She showed me her cabinets which were subject divided and alphabetically arranged, and I have never looked back.

You acquired organisational skills?

And some. I bought a second-hand, four-drawer filing-cabinet, and put it in our dining room. I swapped our dining-suite for a bookcase, a desk and a typing chair, and an old Imperial. I made my own office. Everything looked cheap, cobbled together, but I was serious about it. I read books. I learnt how to label and colour-code. I learnt about stationery, about fine-point pens and HB pencils, paper, envelopes, sticky-tape, cow-glue, paper-clips and hole-punches. I learnt how to speak on the telephone, and write my own proper letters.

What do you recall of your first visit to the firm of Ferguson and Ferguson?

Mr Ferguson patronising me. Me rushing to the ladies', a dozen mirrors reflecting my teary face, my baggy tracksuit.

But he was a good choice?

Yes, it took us a while to click but eventually he asked me to work alongside him, to raise the profile of the case, to put pressure on Peter's Perfect Pies. My office became a campaign headquarters. I wanted my husband, this family, to get its due. It paid off handsomely.

Didn't it? That was a very big award.

Yes, Jenny, it was.

Makeover

Rita watched as Celia moved about the small square kitchen. Celia was wearing a black dress and a dinky black and yellow spotted waistcoat, both bought on Simon's plastic. Her hair was in a French roll. A pair of gold hearts dangled from her ears. She was a woman in dire straits but she didn't look like one, and Rita wanted some of her flair, her friend's never-say-die; Rita wanted back something of what she herself had lost. 'It's hopeless,' Rita said. 'Because he's not interested. He won't push for us, I'm sure.'

'Let's have a cup of tea,' Celia suggested. She took down a box of Economy Red Label, but then put it to one side and prised open a Tupperware container instead. 'Darjeeling or Earl Grey?' she asked.

'Oh ... er ... what's Darjeeling like?'

'Never mind.' Celia pulled two slim paper packets from the Tupperware. 'I've found my favourite. I thought I'd run out. Nicked them from Simon's.' She smiled. 'Nilgiri. You'll love this.'

Behind Celia was a large uncurtained window. It

framed the usual high-rise view. No land. Only grey streaky sky. A pigeon flapped close, its wings and belly almost brushing the pane, and Rita recalled the birdshit on her parents' windows, her mother wearily, angrily, rubbing away at it with a Vileda.

Celia had moved back into her old flat, F34, Speedwell, Crossforth, because Simon had had enough of her. The parting hadn't been amicable. Simon had punched Celia in the eye. He'd thrown her belongings, her frocks and shoes and accessories, and the chiffonier he'd bought her one Christmas, on to his front drive. He'd dropped her from his life, vehemently and finally. He hadn't wanted her forwarding address.

The Council was happy to rent F34 back to Celia. It was an unpopular property, in an unpopular area, and had remained empty throughout her spell in Greenacres. The Council had even redecorated it for her, but succeeded only in making the place appear even more of a bolt-hole than home-sweet-home, the walls a waiting-room beige, the ceilings and skirting a blood-sucked pink. Celia's knick-knacks, the trophies of her time with Simon, loitered dejectedly in the boxy rooms.

Rita shuffled her bottom on the kitchen chair. 'How can you stand it?' she blurted, as the boiling kettle released its valiant whistle. 'This must be such a come-down. It's horrible.'

'Thanks,' Celia said merrily, pouring the water into the teapot. 'But I can't get my knickers in a twist about it. I'll give it a makeover, tart it up with some drapes and stencilling. But really it's just a stop-gap. I won't be here for ever.'

'My God.' Rita buttoned up Celia's silk blouse, then pulled on Celia's linen skirt and zipped it easily, without having to hold her stomach in. 'I've room to spare.'

'You must've lost, what, over two stones?' Celia said.

'Mmm.' Rita felt close to tears. She twirled before the full-length mirror. 'These are just right,' she said. 'Really classy.' But it wasn't the outfit which was getting to her so much as being rid of that tracksuit, her saggy faded gear which smelt of chip-fat and grimy corners. It was being given back a shape. Not the shape she remembered. She was skinny, made gaunt with every worry going, and it didn't really suit her, but even so. She had breasts, she had buttocks. She was still a woman. There was still something there.

'Come on. You haven't got all day.' Celia handed Rita a pair of high-heels. 'Now put these on,' she bossed. 'I know you're a five but we can always pad them with tissue if they feel sloppy.'

Rita obeyed. 'I think they're okay,' she said, wobbling uncertainly.

'Good.' Celia steadied her, then steered her to the dressing-table and sat her down, giving her a cosmetics bag. 'Now for the slap.' Rita looked at the bag. 'Don't be shy,' Celia said, clicking on the dressing-table light. 'Unzip.'

Celia's distinctive perfume, a spicy fragrance, puffed from the bag, and Rita coughed as she searched for some foundation among the pots and palettes of eyeshadow, the lipsticks, blushers, and mascara. Lady Glamour Beige Tone 3. Rita unscrewed the tube. She squirted a dab on to a fingertip.

'No, use one of these,' Celia advised, selecting a snippet of natural sponge from a tray on the table which was filled also with make-up brushes and cotton-wool balls and buds. 'You'll get a smoother finish. Spit on it first.'

'I'm so out of practice,' Rita admitted, taking the sponge, peering at her reflection. 'Christ.' The overhead light was too bright and honest. Rita scanned every illuminated inch of her face, from her forehead to her chin. 'This isn't very flattering. I come off better in the full-length.' She tutted. She couldn't help it. Her skin was no longer an elastic tawny brown but sprinkled with red dots and, here and there, a white spot. She had wrinkles, and half-ovals of bluey-black cupping her eyes. Jesus. She even had a bristle sprouting from the mole on her cheek. It wouldn't be easy.

'This isn't going to be easy,' said Celia. She crouched to examine the bristle. 'I'll get some tweezers to that.'

'Beautiful,' said Celia, unplugging the curling tongs. 'Don't you think?'

'I'm not sure,' Rita replied. The cosmetics made her appear somehow wiped, but she supposed, having everything brush-stroked, the strain and wrinkles disguised, made her easier on the eye, more presentable.

'Well, you are using my colours,' Celia remarked. 'You'd perhaps suit more earthy tones, a browny-orange on your lids, a darker lipstick. You'll have to experiment.'

Rita laughed. 'Celia, I don't have the time.'

'I'm not listening,' Celia said, holding the tongs to Rita's hair.

A warm toasty smell exuded from the metal roller and clip as it clamped in a wave, and it transported Rita, took her back to when she and Celia had preened themselves for Scamps. Every Saturday night. That homely smell, which was more persistent than their perfume even, clinging round them as they queued to get inside the club and queued for its cloakroom, lining up along the glittery mirrored lobby that had reflected Rita over and over and over, that had seemed to confirm her specialness, her potential.

'Well,' said Celia, brushing through the final wave. 'I think this'll open Ferguson's eyes. He'll want to get on your case now.'

'You really think so?' Rita asked.

'I know so,' Celia replied.

Mr Ferguson

I have nothing but respect for Mrs Rita Swales. She has great inner strength and tremendous courage. She refused to be broken by her husband's dreadful accident. Instead she used it to her and her family's advantage. I am not afraid to admit that we would not have got the settlement we did without Mrs Rita Swales's diligence and spirit. She is a remarkable woman.

The Present

The sun has shifted and no longer shines directly into Rita's Housesitting Service. It slides in from the side, through the wedged-open door. New and more subtle shadows play across the office floor, and a star of light adorns one of the leaflet racks. A gentle breeze whispers round the room. It is cooler. Rita, feeling less sweaty and sticky, sits at her desk talking on the phone to Celia.

'It's the cream dress with the scooped neck,' Rita tells her friend.

'Oh, that's a good choice,' Celia replies.

'I think so,' says Rita. 'It's a day dress, knee-length, but a special one.'

'Oh, yes,' Celia confirms. 'It shows off your assets. Very important.'

'Tools of the trade,' Rita says.

'Oh yes,' Celia confirms.

Rita is happy, as usual, to hear from her friend. She experiences a rush like the rush she feels when flirting. Celia is a reminder of Crossforth, of Rita's past, but that isn't the attraction. Rather, Rita enjoys Celia for her cold-shouldering of things long gone, for the way she embraces now, hungrily, like nothing else matters. Celia is the oldest swinger in Cranley. She is Fun with a capital F. And she lightens Rita's load.

'Well, I'll go for my red number,' Celia says.

'Popular,' Rita comments. 'I had Captain Salcott in earlier. She was wearing red.'

'Lovely.'

'A rhinestone jacket.'

'Super.'

'She was mincing like she'd a carrot up her arse, and she was panting after Collis.' Rita hears Celia tap the receiver, a habit of hers.

'But of course,' Celia says, drumming her nails. 'Salcott likes a sob story, especially if he's handsome. Is he coming tonight?'

'I don't know.' Rita sighs. 'He's being standoffish. The usual.'

'Give him Salcott's number then. They're made for each other.'

'Celia!'

'Well, I don't know how you put up with him.'

'That should do it,' says Rita. She smiles at her assistants, tousled and flushed from their carrying, securing and rearranging. They've taken the computers and printer, the in-trays and out-trays, the desk-tidies and the Rotadex through to the staff quarters. They've locked the filing-cabinets and desk drawers. They've pushed the desks together to form a long table which they've draped with paper cloths. They've distributed the flowers at regular intervals along the table. And Nolene, who lost the toss, has Hoovered the carpet and sponged down the sofa.

'Can we have a rest now, Mrs Swales?' the junior asks.

Rita surveys their handiwork. It's looking good. The agency is roomier now. There's space for guests to stand and chat, to sit and chat; there's space for clumping and for mingling.

'Mrs Swales?' Nolene persists.

'Nope! No time.' Rita eyes the caterer's van parked outside the agency. The van doors are open and uniformed figures are leaning into it, backsides protruding. 'Food is here,' she says.

'Oh good.' Philippa claps her hands, and Nolene glares at her, then a tall man enters the agency, dressed in blue trousers, a white chef's jacket and blue peaked cap.

'Food For Thought,' the man declares, striding quickly, expertly balancing six plates stacked with sandwiches along his long thin arms. He is pursued by a tiny woman in a navy frock holding an enormous nibbles tray, and a Neanderthal lugging two large crates.

'Wine too,' observes Philippa.

'And fancy water,' the Neanderthal gruffly confirms, looking about for somewhere to dump his load.

'Make space for the booze, Nolene,' Rita orders. 'Shift that vase.'

Nolene does as she is told and the Neanderthal – 'Alley Hup!' – swings the crates on to the table. 'Ta,' he says, his eyes meeting with Nolene's breasts.

Nolene takes a deep breath, inflating *her* assets, and Rita watches. She's not sure about Nolene. She suspects a sad episode in her early years, a rejection which has hardened her heart. Because the girl's more often moody than she's warm and, even when presenting her charms like now, there's a tackle-me-if-you-dareness about her. Rita wonders if she should introduce her to one of her boys. Not Graham, though, because he's engaged, and not Ben because he's too young and just as messed-up.

Perhaps Jimmy. He's fun. He might soften her. She'll have to think about it.

The tall man in the chef's jacket re-enters the agency. He carries a gâteau sprinkled with coconut and silver balls, and a transparent bowl of unnaturally shiny fruit. 'Any jelly?' Bill shouts, following behind.

Bill nips Nolene's backside and, as she twists to complain, Bill mouths 'Sorry', weaving round her, apologising further with a smile.

Rita holds a hand to her chest. So he's returned, and he's wearing his party tie.

'Hello Gorgeous,' he whispers.

'Decrepit,' she replies.

'May I?' He takes her arm, running his fingers along her skin, toying with the warm metal of her bracelets. 'I told you I'd be back.'

'You've told me a lot of things,' she says.

'I know.' He lets go of her arm. 'But I've got something for you.' He fumbles in his jacket pocket.

'Oh.'

'Here.' He proffers a box. 'A present.'

Rita accepts the box, catching a whiff of Bill's breath. 'I hope you've not been silly,' she warns. The porgy has gone, replaced by minty toothpaste.

'It's to celebrate your anniversary,' he says. 'I hope you don't mind?'

'Depends what it is.'

Rita is relieved the jewellery box isn't ring-sized. It is much larger. It is covered with crimson velvet. It is stamped with a gold crown and two acorns. Rita recognises the insignia. 'Hoffmans,' she murmurs, no longer relieved.

She turns the box over in her hands. It could be empty of course. Or it could be filled with something plastic, a lucky bag bracelet, a joke. It could be a joke. Rita clicks the box open – 'Christ' – and sees what she does not want to see, a typical Hoffmans' performance, a far-from-a-joke brooch, a spiral of silver resembling a target, expensively fat on a pad of red silk. It must've cost a bomb. Rita shakes her head; and the opal marking the brooch's bullseye glimmers a creamy yellow, a pale blue, its milkiness washing over her, showing her, declaring to her that Bill is in earnest. He isn't about to give up. This is serious.

Bill's chunky finger jabs the opal. 'Your birthstone,' he tells her.

'Unlucky for some,' Rita says, feeling hot, feeling cold.

'It's probably a bit over-the-top,' Bill continues, playing with Rita's bangles again, nervously now, jingling them, their music almost lost to the toings and froings of the Food for Thoughters and the chink-chink of wine-glasses. 'But I wanted to get you something special.'

'It's a lot over-the-top,' Rita says. Then. 'Girls!' she shouts at Nolene and Philippa who are pulling the glasses from foam-lined cartons and plonking them on the table. 'Careful now. We have to pay for breakages.'

'But you'll accept it?' Bill persists. He takes Rita's wrist, holding it between a finger and thumb, drawing back her attention.

'I need to get changed,' Rita replies.

'I was hoping it would go with your dress. You'll wear it with your dress?'

'Okay,' Rita tells him, because she cannot help it, because the brooch is very beautiful, because... 'I will.'

Arriving

Rita was shaking. She could barely turn the key in the Yale. Come on. Come on. She swung the door open and belted inside. 'I've got it! I've got it!' She waved the cheque in the air. 'Here it is! Here we are!' She took a sideways swerve past Collis's bedding, the quilt and pillows bundled in the hall until night-time. 'No more dossing on the couch,' she shouted as she stormed the kitchen. 'No more—' Rita made a pinching motion with her free hand. 'None of that. No scrimping. We're in the money!'

Collis smiled. He was leaning against the sink, filling the kettle with water. 'Tea?' he asked.

'Bugger tea,' said Rita. 'Let's get this banked! Let's go shopping!'

'Calm down.' Collis put the kettle on the drainer and turned off the tap.

'I'm not plugging that in for you,' Rita said. 'There's no way I'm letting go of this.' Rita kissed the cheque. 'This little beauty.'

'But you're going to have to,' Collis replied. 'It's in my name.'

‘A mere technicality.’ Rita was beside her husband. The sink unit was taking most of his weight, his crutches under his armpits like scaffolding.

‘Big word,’ Collis said. ‘Technicality.’

‘I’m full of them,’ Rita replied.

Collis stared at Rita. ‘Yes,’ he said. ‘It’s rubbed off. La-di-da Ferguson.’

‘Paid off,’ said Rita. She pulled the cheque taut between her hands and showed it to her husband. ‘Look. Count the noughts.’

Collis let out a breath. ‘Jesus.’ His dark eyes began to fill. ‘It’s real.’

‘I know.’ Rita stroked her husband’s arm, and the mirror on the far wall caught the movement.

She looked across, and there they were. Collis and Rita reflected. Their heads and shoulders. As Collis took in the cheque Rita took in her appearance, her made-up face, her gently waved hair; all her own work and not too bad. But soon she’d be paying professionals to spruce her. Soon she wouldn’t have to consult Celia about earthy tones and what to do with her fringe. Soon everything would change. ‘I bet you’re hard,’ she whispered.

Collis glanced up from the cheque, and he met Rita’s smile in the mirror, and he smiled too, and it was as if no damage had been done, they looked like they used to look, years ago, in the mirror, from their shoulders up, the perfect couple.

Rita pressed the cheque against Collis’s chest. Then, slowly, she slithered it down.

‘Careful, Rita,’ he said. ‘Don’t rip it.’

But she was right. He was hard.

‘The boys could come back any—’

‘Shush.’ Rita pushed the cheque into his trouser pocket. ‘A house,’ she said. ‘Then a business. Then a party.’

Collis looked down at his wife as she unzipped his trousers.

'My name is Rita,' she said.

'Collis,' he replied, and he edged from the sink, his crutches supporting him.

'Collis.' Rita's knees met the cold floor. 'A bungalow first,' she murmured, 'A big one in Greenacres,' and took him into her mouth.

A New Home.

A one-off built in the 1920s beside Greenacres' Methodist chapel. A white and spacious bungalow. The boys had a bedroom each. The kitchen looked out on to a long back garden which was half lawn and flowers, half vegetable plot.

'We'll sink a pond there,' Rita said, pointing to the bared earth dotted with remnants of winter cabbage and brussels gone to seed.

'No,' Collis replied. 'I'll take that on. I'll need something to do.'

A Business.

The Iced Diamond stood outside the opened rear door of Rita's newly purchased business premises. Rita knelt on the rough concrete of the car park and scrubbed at the fridge's interior, pushing her J-Cloth into its mouldy corners, rubbing away the yellowy-green streaks on the egg tray.

'How's it going?' asked Collis.

'Oh.' Rita looked up to see her husband. 'Fine,' she said. 'And you?' Collis and the boys were working in the back room of the property.

'Graham's unblocking the sink, and Jim's fixing the skirting in the loo.'

'And Donny and Ben?' Rita wiped her hand across her brow. She'd tucked her hair beneath a scarf, and was wearing her old tracksuit. She disliked being in her scruff again, this dressing-down, but she knew it wouldn't be for much longer.

'They're opening a tin of paint,' said Collis.

'It takes two?'

'It's stuck tight,' Collis explained. 'They're using spoons.'

'They should try a screwdriver,' Rita suggested.

Collis looked from her to the wheelie bins at the far end of the car park. 'I'm supervising the boys,' he eventually replied.

A Party.

Rita stood at the patio doors and watched the bonfire on Collis's vegetable patch. Her sons had constructed it for the price of an evening's session at Cranley's bowling alley. They'd used Collis's garden refuge, some packing crates and newspaper, piling these around Rita's and Collis's old bed: the buckled and stained stripy mattress, the double divan base with its handy storage drawers.

The stuff was dry and burning a treat. Adults and children had gathered round the blaze; mainly adults, enjoying the freedom of being out, coatless, in early winter. Rita could see their chattering silhouettes, the clouds of frosty breath, and she could sense their excitement. This was going so well. Rita took a swig of her wine, congratulating herself, toasting her future.

Ben ran up the garden. Rita saw him pushing through the darkness towards her.

'Mum! Mum! Dad's doing the rocket!'

Rita grabbed her son as he fell smack to her body, and a splosh of wine jumped from her glass, staining his shirt.

'Mum! Oh Mum! That's my new top!' Ben rubbed and spat at the mark, and Rita span him around.

'Don't worry yourself Ben.' She pointed him back at the bonfire. 'We'll get another one. Now go and tell your father he needs his head seeing to, and try and find Celia's latest, or that big video store man, anyone. Find someone else to light the fireworks. And Ben: Catherine Wheels first, rockets last.'

Rita circulated, networking, charming, laughing louder than the Jumping Jacks, and she felt herself glow, growing bigger and bigger, flush with it all.

Then she spied Collis, standing some way from the explosives, stork-like and alone, in the furthest corner of their garden.

'Are you okay, love?'

Rita turned the words over, sipping from her wine. 'Are you okay, love?' But she didn't go near him, not then, or for the rest of the evening. Because it would have been like sucking helium from her and this, her special night.

'Are we okay, love?'

Collis.

Rita.

'Are we okay?'

Ben

I don't like to think about Mum. Whenever I think about her I get a pain in the head. Sophie, my girlfriend, hates her. She says she's a fat, ugly cow, always poking her nose in where it's not wanted. Sophie's from New Horizons. We used to live round the corner from her. Her brother works at the pie factory, on the box-and-wrap line where Dad had his accident.

Sophie and I started going out last year. Dad gets bored stuck at home and he rang for a taxi and took me along for the ride. He was going to go to Crossforth, where he was born, but he changed his mind and we ended up at Sophie's. Dad and Sophie's brother went to the pub and that left me with her. She made the first move. She said she'd always liked me.

Mum went mental. 'What do you want a girlfriend for?' she shouted. 'You've got your exams soon! Don't throw it all away!' Mum wants me to go to university. She wants a degree in the family, something else to boast about to the neighbours and those creeps she gets at her parties. She's never satisfied. She's pushy and bossy, and she's really two-faced.

I invited Sophie round for tea. Dad cooked it, ham and chips, and Mum arrived, late from work as usual, as we were finishing. She barely said a word. She was polite but she was ice. She waited until Sophie had gone home, and then she couldn't keep it in, going on about my school-work again, going on about Sophie's weight or lack of it, how she's too skinny, her face too ratty. 'She's not a beauty, is she?' she said. 'She's got nothing about her,' she said. 'What do you see in her? I hope it's not what I think it is? I hope there's more to her than that.'

Dad says Mum only wants the best for me. But then Dad always makes excuses for Mum. He's soft on her and won't accept we're far happier at home without her.

'What I do with Sophie is my business,' I told Mum. 'You stick to your business, and I'll stick to mine.'

And I will. Because Sophie's fun. She's the first girl who's let me.

On the Throne

Rita sits on the throne and opens her new pack of stockings. She unfolds them, removes the piece of card separating the legs. She throws the packaging into the bin, and rolls the stockings on, smoothing them over her calves, her knees, then – standing, stepping into her high-heels – over her substantial thighs. She secures the creamy lacy tops to her suspender belt. She sits back down and fishes in her handbag for her mobile. She presses the digits for home.

'Yes,' Collis answers.

'That was quick,' Rita replies.

'I've just finished a call,' Collis says.

'To Speed U's?'

'No.' There is a pause; Collis could be scratching his head or fingering his stump as he sits in the hall by the phone. 'I was ordering something for the garden, actually.'

'Such as?'

'A few things.'

'Oh.'

Rita crosses her legs. She stares at the toilet walls which are varnished tongue-and-groove, the skirting and towel-rail stained bottle-green, the mirror with stencilled ivy-leaves on its frame. Celia's influence, of course. 'Some clients will want a pee,' she told Rita. 'A natty loo is better for business than a hole in the ground.' Rita uncrosses her legs. She listens to Collis's silence.

'If you're not careful,' she wants to tell him. 'You'll lose me, you will. There's somebody who's really keen on me, and wants to make me happy.' But she says nothing. She looks down at the package in the bin. Collis likes her in underwear. She will try this. 'Guess what I'm—'

'Ben gave me your message,' Collis says. 'He's in a nasty mood. Did you upset him?'

Sod it. Rita crosses her legs. 'I didn't upset him.' She puts the phone to her other ear. 'You know what he's like.'

'Do I?'

'He's your son.'

Another silence. And Rita isn't going to break it. Not this time. She stands. She puts the mobile on the cistern, and reaches for her party frock hanging from the hook on the back of the toilet door. She takes the Hoffmans' brooch box from her cosmetics case, and only raises the mobile to her ear again when she hears the fuzzy faraway burbling of her husband's voice.

'Rita? You still there?'

'Of course,' she replies.

'I'm sorry.'

'That's good.' But really the apology's come too late. Rita feels it has come too late.

'Are you about ready?' Collis then asks.

'Yes.'

'I'll join you as soon as I can.'

You will? Rita shakes her head, disbelieving, then says, 'Got to go. Someone's calling me.'

Rita opens the brooch box. She stares at Bill's gift. The swirl of silver, the opal in the brooch's eye which is not one deep wedge of brilliance like a ruby or emerald but more transitory, flecked with moving colour, its pale blues unfixed, its muted yellows fluid. The kind of stone which is open to interpretation, which can't commit. He chose it, he said, because it's her birthstone. He chose it, perhaps, because he saw her in the opal, how she can be one thing then another, then both things together, cold then hot, cold and hot together, inviting then withdrawing, inviting and withdrawing.

'I am in love with you,' he said.

'Bill, shut up,' she replied.

Rita helped Ernest to sort through Agnes's belongings after her death. He was going to dump the lot but somehow Rita persuaded him to keep a few mementos. He chose oddities like Agnes's cleaning mat, a packet of her hairgrips, and her housekeeping purse. He passed the jewellery on to Rita: the Saint Christopher, the pair of fake gold clip-ons, her rings. He pointed to the clip-ons and said, 'I got her those when we moved into the flat. She never put them on, felt they were too fancy. You know how she was. She kept them, I suppose, because they reminded her.'

'Of what?' asked Rita. She was sitting at the kitchen table. Ernest was opposite her. They were sitting facing each other, alone, together, just the two of them. Rita looked at her father and waited. He clicked open and refastened the housekeeping purse, clicked it open and closed it. 'What did they remind her of?' Rita said. 'Dad?'

'Things,' Ernest snapped, standing up. 'Just things.'

He ran his hand along the worktop which was shiny and smelt of cleanser, of Agnes still. He fished inside a cupboard, and pulled out a pan, set it on the cooker. He looked into the hallway, agitated, restless. 'Where is she?' he breathed.

'Gone,' Rita said. 'She's gone.'

Rita puts the brooch box on the cistern alongside her mobile. She takes her party dress out of its dry-cleaning bag and holds it to the light. Its surface is liquid and silky; the bodice embroidered with scrolls and trefoils, the decoration a shade darker than the fabric beneath. Rita's fingers trace a scroll. She loves this frock. She wants to think only about this frock.

Rita pulls the frock over her head, wriggles into it, feeling it fall and fit shamelessly to her flesh. She zips it up, and lifts the hem to straighten the underskirt beneath. She runs her fingers around its neckline. The neckline is scooped, immodest, designed to reveal her breasts. It pushes them up and moulds them so they appear to be spilling, on the brink of exposing the dizzying brown of her nipples. Tasteless yet tasteful. Discreet yet indiscreet.

Rita dabs a little powder on her chest, then returns the puff to her cosmetics case. She takes a tube of white highlighter, squirts a smidgen of the jelly on to a fingertip, and works it into her cleavage. She checks her face in the mirror.

She doesn't look as drawn as earlier. (The patch must be working. Thank God.) There's just some touching-up required. She redefines her mouth with a red pencil, her eyebrows with a fawny-brown. She brushes and fluffs her hair, her gold bracelets jingling with the movement. She takes them off. She tucks them into her case, clips a pair of silver studs to her ear-lobes, and then she picks up the Hoffmans' box.

Her heart skips a beat. She lifts the box lid, aware of her breasts rising, lifting too, as she looks at the brooch again. Bill's gift. What will it remind her of in two, three, or twenty years' time? Their flirtation? The fifth anniversary of Rita's Housesitting Service? Or? Rita shivers. Or will it remind her of a move she has yet to make, a leap he feels she ought to take?

Rita cups the brooch in the palm of her hand, the skin of her right breast nudging the base of her thumb. The brooch feels hot like somebody has polished and polished it with the corner of a cloth. Her wedding ring had felt exactly the same. Rita remembers Collis taking her finger and sliding the band on, and the metal burning her, melting on to and into her.

'I will always love you,' she had said to him. 'And I will never ever leave you.'

I will never ever leave you. Rita drops the brooch box into her cosmetics case, and bundles the dry-cleaning bag into the bin under the sink.

The Queen

Rita makes an entrance. She glides elegantly, head held high, past the partition, into her office proper.

'Oh, Mrs Swales!' exclaims Philippa. 'You look lovely.'

'Thank you.'

'I'll second that,' says Bill from across the room. He leans back against a filing-cabinet as if steadying himself, and he lets out a low slow whistle.

'You still here?' Rita snaps.

Bill straightens, surprised.

'Won't Josie be missing you?' Rita persists.

'No.' He is cautious. 'Josie won't be missing me.'

'Mr Henley's been keeping us company,' Philippa explains.

'Yes, Mr Henley's been telling us all about his wife,' Nolene adds. The girl smiles a little smile and Rita thinks of Ben, how he behaves when he talks of someone he doesn't like, considers stupid. 'Mr Henley's been discussing qualifications,' the girl continues.

'I see,' Rita says.

'Mr Henley thinks they're very important.'

'Okay, Nolene. That's enough.' Rita takes a deep breath. 'So—'

The agency door has been closed, and no traffic sounds, no heels clattering on pavements, no shouts or cries or snatches of conversation, no barking dogs, no sounds intrude. Rita's office is a sealed-off space. Waiting.

'We've put the empty boxes and rubbish by the wheelie-bins,' Philippa informs.

'Hush,' says Rita, and she starts to circle the room.

She takes a tray of canapés from one end of the food and drinks' table, places it at the other. She fusses with droopy carnations, regroups wine glasses, smoothes a creased napkin. She picks a fern sprig off the floor. She closes, then opens her eyes.

She's surrounded by light. She spreads her arms wide, splaying her fingers, aware of her assistants, of Bill watching, all of him – leathery skin, big nose, thick neck, chest, trunk, hefty thighs – watching. She holds her palms upwards, and she turns slowly. Rita's Housesitting Service. She turns slowly, weighing her queendom, finding it balanced and to her liking. 'Tremendous,' she declares. 'Thank you.'

'Good,' Nolene says. 'Now, maybe, I can get a go in the loo.' The girl lumbers to the staff quarters, clumsily shouldering the balloon-covered partition. The balloons lift up, and then, like a lover's waning smile, drift sadly down.

'Jesus!' Rita exclaims suddenly. 'Lemon slices!'

'Oh, sorry, yes,' blurts Philippa. 'I forgot.'

'Well get shifting. Chop! Chop! We're running out of time.'

Bill and Rita. Alone in the office.

Bill places one big foot before the other as if he is

about to curtsey. 'Thank you for wearing it,' he whispers, leaning towards her.

Rita fingers the brooch on her bodice. It is still warm. 'Thank you for giving me it,' she replies.

'We're being very polite.'

'Yes.'

'Well,' he says. 'It's ex. Nolene made a mistake. My wife is no longer my wife. She's my ex.'

'I know.'

'Good.'

'I've always known.'

'Good.' Bill strokes her wrist. 'No bangles,' he observes.

'No bangles,' she confirms. Then. 'Don't.'

A taxi is outside the agency. Rita pulls from Bill, seeing its colours, the purple hood, the blue doors, the inscription *We Can SPEED U Anywhere* on its side. Rita's sandals catch on the coir matting as she puts distance between her and Bill, as she watches the taxi driver lean into the back of his car to help his passenger out. Collis?

'What's wrong?' asks Bill.

No. Not Collis. Only a hugely pregnant woman in striped dungarees.

Rita looks at Bill. 'It's a quarter to five, that's what's wrong,' she says. 'Guests will be arriving.' Bill stares. She shrugs. She pushes a hand through her hair. 'Got to get a move on,' she says.

'Of course.' Bill continues to stare. 'Later?' he then asks.

Rita nods, and the nod is barely perceptible, one she can pretend never happened, if she wants, if she decides. Christ. 'We need music.' What's she doing? 'We need,' she raises her voice. 'We need those lemon slices!'

'I'll do the music,' Bill offers. 'Okay?' He reaches out, squeezes Rita's shoulder. She flinches. 'Okay?' he says again, removing his hand and holding it in the air, showing there's nothing, absolutely nothing, up his sleeve.

'If you want.'

'I want. Now.' He looks about him. 'Where are your CDs?'

Rita points, and he goes to the rack. 'Quite a selection,' he says. 'What do you fancy?' He thumbs through them, their plastic cases clicking against each other. 'Something quiet to begin with? I think so. Parties should start quiet, then—'

But Rita's stopped listening. She's seen a ghost. Suddenly. From the corner of her eye. Outside. The taxi has gone, and there, across the road, is the ghost. Rita hurries to the agency door, keeping track of the weary woman, wearing a housecoat, carrying a mop, a bucket, a mat shaped like a kidney; a woman with a bulky awkward shape and rounded shoulders, a cleaning lady's stoopiness.

'Jesus! Mary!'

Doreen is at the door. The sun halos her modest perm, her face glares whitely through the glass. Am I too early? she mouths.

'No. No.' Rita composes herself. 'No. Come in. Come in,' she says, opening the door. 'I didn't see you there. I was miles away.'

'Oh.' Doreen blinks her puppyish eyes and, as she does so, Rita notices the crusted cut across the bridge of her nose, and Rita concentrates on this small ugliness, focuses down on it, irritated by it, but, at this moment, grateful for it too. Rita points to the injury.

'I'll get you some concealer for that,' she says.

Wreaths

Rita had had to recalculate her prospects because her business was taking an age to pull in the clients. Perhaps by the fourth year it would provide the income she'd anticipated. Perhaps by then she could risk spending the remainder of the compensation money on a small place in Greenacres for her parents, for Agnes.

'What do you want to do that for?' Collis asked.

'Because Mum deserves somewhere nice.'

Rita imagined Agnes opening her doughy arms to Greenacres' pure air, feeling it with her scrubbed fingertips. Her mother would surely marvel at the litter-free streets, the regular pavements, the shiny grass of the verges, the polished pebbles in the driveways. Such an environment would do wonders for her health, would wipe away her defeatism, would make her see life and herself, perhaps even Rita, differently.

'Forget it,' said Collis. 'You're dreaming.'

Rita's mother died two months later. She died in her bed in the flat in Crossforth. She'd been ill for some time but

Rita never expected the end to come so suddenly. She hadn't even mentioned the possibility of a house.

Which left only Ernest, wiry, thin-lipped, standing rigid by his wife's graveside, no wreath bought in his name. Rita felt cheated. She wouldn't be spending any money on him. He deserved punishment, nothing but a paying-back for his treatment of Agnes, for his belligerence and black moods, for his harshness to Rita, for his behaviour at her wedding, for being her father, for being.

A few weeks later Ernest said, 'I want to move somewhere people will look after me like your mother did. I want you to sort it so I don't have to cook my own meals or make my own bed or do my own shopping and cleaning. I'm too old to start doing all that. I want to put my feet up and I want to be out of Crossforth because I want wallpaper which stays on the walls.'

The brochure was printed on recycled card and in its introduction were the words *ethos*, *culture*, *collective*, *humanist*, and the phrases *personal development*, *equal opportunities*, *creative play*, *self-determination*. There were paintings and poems by the residents. There were photographs of rickety women dancing round a Maypole, wrinkly men drumming on tom-toms. It was exactly what Rita was looking for. Ernest would hate it. She booked an appointment to visit.

Rest-A-While was out in the country on land once owned by the third Earl of Cranley. The Earl's mansion held Rest-A-While's offices, dining hall, library, and clubroom. There were bedrooms on the ground floor for disabled residents, while the fitter ones lived in insulated pine chalets dotted round the estate and its lake.

It all looked strait-laced, respectable. There were no outward signs of hippyishness, of windchimes and nut burgers. There was nothing but grandeur. The mansion had been stone-washed, its drive cobbled, its surroundings landscaped with conifers and lawn. The chalets resembled plush Scandinavian holiday homes. Ernest would take one look and be wanting to move there.

Because Ernest liked to swank, he liked to show off, and he took every opportunity, happily hijacking and parading anything remotely boastworthy, anything with the slightest connection to him. Reflected glory. He was into it. Rita knew. Because he'd begun to brag about her, especially since she'd been featured in the *Cranley Gazette*. He'd even hinted that he'd like to come to one of her parties.

So Rita bought Ernest a pub lunch and oiled him with a few whiskies, and then she took him to Rest-A-While. A smile crossed his face as he viewed the mansion's exterior, the marble framing its front door and the gargoyles projecting from its gutterings. Rita pointed out the coat of arms carved in stone above the entrance and she told Ernest everything she knew about the third Earl, about his fabulous wealth, his innumerable servants. She showed Ernest the lake and the little island in its middle complete with turreted folly, and she said, 'All this could be yours, Dad. You could live here, on the Earl's estate, surrounded by all this.'

'Just wait until I tell the neighbours,' he said. 'It's better than Snob Land,' he said. 'They'll be green.'

'I've done it!' Rita could hardly contain herself. Ernest was ready to give his flat back to the Council, pack his bags, commit himself to Rest-A-While without quizzing its governing collective or any of the residents, without looking inside the place even. 'Everything I touch,' she told Collis. 'Everything's going right for me. Ernest'll be shacked-up there before he'll realise. The tie-dye workshops. T'ai'-chi by the lake in the early mornings. I can't wait.'

'Don't be so juvenile,' said Collis.

'What?' Rita stared at her husband. Why must he be

so negative, so unsupportive? Why couldn't he enjoy her success? 'What do you mean?'

'He's an old man,' said Collis. 'An easy target now. It'll serve you right if he settles in.'

Which Ernest did. Straight away. He polished his name-plaque on his chalet door. He put a pot of geraniums on the chalet's veranda and rocked in his rocker there, watching the sun rise over the lake. He weeded the organic vegetable garden, picked caterpillars off the cabbage leaves. He learnt to cha-cha-cha and shake cocktails. He helped Rest-A-While's dreadlocked chef prepare a TVP roast. And he was happy to call his own special carer by her first name and always thanked her for her kindness: for fixing the tie in his pyjama bottoms, for colouring his hair from its orangey-grey to Reagan black, for rubbing scented oils into his knotted shoulders. The tension dropped from him, and he even discarded his old Timex, began wearing his digital. He was happy in his new home.

Rita could hardly stomach it. 'That old bastard,' she said.

Party On

Rita squeezes through the half-opened partition into the office staff quarters, and the noise from the party pursues her: Celine Dion giving it everything, the clatter of cutlery and crockery and chatter, the effusive hellos! of newly arrived guests, the laughter accompanying the shaking of hands, the sudden – feigned or genuine – exclamations of surprise:

'What lovely decorations!'

'Gorgeous flowers!'

'Stupendous inflatables!'

'Marvellous spread!'

Rita unlocks and opens the agency's back door. The outside rushes to greet her with a wind-blown sheet of smell: the warm heady odour of car park and road, of petrol and exhaust, of the restaurant kitchens and overflowing wheelie-bins, of late afternoon.

'What's this?'

'Oh!' Rita glances quick behind her. She sees Bill, his white shirt, the knot of his snazzy tie.

'Sorry,' says Bill.

‘So you should be.’

‘You’re very jumpy.’

‘Yes.’ Rita stares out at the parked cars, their wing-mirrors glinting with light, and she wills him to go.

He runs a finger down her spine, drawing a hot line from her neck to her waist. ‘What’s the matter?’

‘Don’t,’ she snaps.

‘Has something upset you?’ he asks. ‘Have I upset you?’

‘No.’

A Citroën pulls into the car park, comes to a halt by Mr Fruity Man’s hideous green van. The driver gets out. A young woman, a possible party-goer. Rita moves from her admirer.

‘Well, what is it then?’ Bill sticks close. Rita can hear him. He breathes the laboured breaths of a slightly heavy man. Rita shifts again. ‘Collis?’ he persists.

The young woman opens the Citroën’s passenger doors. Two boys clamber out and a little whimpering girl dressed in pink. The woman lifts the girl and holds her to her chest as she leans into the Citroën’s boot, removing one shopping-bag, then another. The woman is no party-goer, Rita can see this now. Her hair is scraped into a pony-tail, her blue baggy skirt rises on a breeze, displaying her bare pale thighs, her greying knickers. Her boys start to fight and she shouts at them, ‘Christian! Joseph! Enough!’

‘I’m going to have to phone him,’ Rita then says.

Nobody answering?

Will you go. Let me get on with it.

He’s probably on his way if nobody’s answering.

Is that so?

Would that please you? Do you want him to be on his way?

People are expecting him to be here.

And do you want him to be here?

Please.
Because I don't think you do.

Rita walks back through the staff quarters, re-enters her office. It is packed. The front door is wedged open and people are spilling on to the street. A taxi draws up – Rita takes in a breath – but it isn't a Speed U and Joanna Holland is its fare. Rita pours herself a glass of white wine, downs it in one. But it does nothing to quench her thirst, to cool the sweaty heat which is pressing against her, to blot out Bill, his bulky shoulders, as he moves from her, pushing into the bodies crowding the buffet.

'Oh, Mrs Swales, there you are.' Philippa appears, flicking her hair from her eyes. She is flushed, her silky skin glows. A portly gent closely tails her. 'I must introduce you. This man—'

'Mr Cornelius Abbot, at your service,' interrupts the man, stepping forward, popping a cocktail sausage into his ladylike mouth. 'From Haywood Press,' he continues, his molars crushing the sausage as he speaks.

Rita sees the meat flick round his mouth, and she thinks of her sons, of how she used to reproach them for talking while eating. 'Close up,' she used to say. 'Now. This very minute. It's bad manners.' She decides to show her disapproval. She will not shake Mr Abbot's hand.

'Well, this man, Mr Cornelius Abbot.' Philippa is persistent, she's eager to tell. 'Well, Mr Cornelius Abbot is prepared to give us a 30 per cent discount on fan-fold leaflets.'

'He is?' says Rita. Ah.

'I am.' Cornelius Abbot smiles, a snatch of sausage caught between his front teeth. 'And 35 per cent on A5 two-colour fliers.'

'Thirty-five per cent?' says Rita.

Mr Cornelius Abbot nods, and Rita wipes her right hand on a serviette and holds it out. Invitingly.

Joanna Holland approaches. She wears a dazzling white dress which clings tightly to her bony frame. She's tucked her hair behind her ears to show off a pair of diamanté droplets. 'Hello, Mrs Swales,' she says. 'What a turn-out. You must be pleased.'

'Mmm.' Rita nods. Joanna is perfumed, sweet-smelling, and Rita smiles – so, the woman does wash – it bodes well.

'I've been reading that magazine article,' Joanna remarks. 'It's quite in-depth for a glossy, isn't it? A rounded portrait. It's given me a real insight.'

'It has?' Rita pours herself another glass of wine, and she waits for Joanna to say what she knows she wants to say, what everybody eventually says. What an awful thing to have happened to your husband. How did you cope? How does he cope? Your marriage must be very strong to have survived all that. You must really love each other. Though I expect the money helped. It was a lot. Wasn't it?

But Nolene muscles in before Joanna can continue. 'Oh hello!' Nolene clutches a melon slice in one hand, a tankard of something brown and frothy in the other. She smiles at Joanna. 'What lovely earrings!' she enthuses.

'Thank you.' Joanna eyes Nolene, from her hair to her breasts to the swirly rainbow hem of her frock.

And Rita makes her escape. 'There's something I must do,' she says to Nolene, looking at the girl, wondering if she's slewed already since she seems uncharacteristically gushy, excited. 'Can you take care of Ms Holland?'

'Of course, Boss,' Nolene replies. 'You can rely on me.'

Rita turns for the partition as a camera flash goes off, as Doreen comes from the loo.

'Mrs Swales—' Doreen stands before Rita. She fingers the graze on her nose, rubbing the concealer from it. 'The Gallaghers have left a big pile of ironing right in the middle of their kitchen floor.'

'You know the rules,' Rita snaps.

'But—'

'You're a sitter, not a maid.'

The photographer for the *Gazette* stands gibbon-like, bouncing and swaying on his feet, knees bent. He looks over his camera. 'If you can bunch together a bit. Mrs Swales, move closer in.'

'Do we have to do this now?' she asks.

'Come on, Rita.' Bill puts his arm round her shoulders. He draws her near, gives her a squeeze.

'And raise your wine-glasses,' the photographer-primate calls. 'Love-ly.' He takes four shots, his camera flash firing more balls of explosive light.

'Wow!' exclaims a tipsy Celia hanging on to Bill's other arm, clutching it tight. 'Fame! Fortune!'

'Nice one,' says the photographer. He lets his camera dangle by the leather strap around his neck, and pulls a pencil and notepad from his front jeans' pocket.

'You want my address, officer?' asks Celia.

'Just your names.'

'Well, you know who I am,' says Rita.

The photographer quickly scribbles on his pad. 'And you're?'

'He's the manager of the video shop.' Celia pats Bill's backside. 'He's called Bill Henley.'

'And *you* are?' the photographer asks, as Celia sashays towards him.

'I'm Mrs Swales's best friend.' Celia strokes the photographer's camera strap with a long red fingernail. 'I'm a freelance stylist. I'm a Miss, that's MISS Celia Taylor, and I'm very photogenic.'

'He's not coming then?' Celia says.

'Haven't a clue.' Rita removes a dead-head from a vase by the nibbles tray. She chucks it under the table. Out of sight. 'I phoned and there was no answer, so I assumed he was on his way. But that was ages ago. Now I really need to find out what's going off.' She unzips her handbag, rummages inside. 'But I keep getting distracted.'

'It's called a party.' Celia takes a sip of wine. 'Your party.'

'Mmm.' Rita locates her mobile.

'And Collis is doing his usual, fucking it up for you.' Celia raps her nails against the bowl of her wine-glass. Then, 'Excuse!' She grabs the wrist of the photographer as he passes by. She smiles. 'I've a suggestion,' she tells him. 'Me in this gorgeous red number on the lime-green sofa. Brilliant colours.'

'Black and white film,' he says.

Me again.

Yes.

How are you now?

I can't settle.

He doesn't deserve you.

Don't.

Please. Give me a chance. Give yourself a chance.

Rita leans against the agency's back wall. She presses the mobile's key-pad, hearing the numbers inside her head as she does so. Greenacres 420 4303.

She breathes in the stewy air. She gulps it in as the phone rings and rings. Then. At last. Rita hears her eldest son, home from work.

'Yes?'

'Graham, it's Mum. Is Dad there?'

'He is. He's in the kitchen, wearing his suit, his tie, but he won't budge. I can't get a word out of him. What's up?'

Stevie Richmond's gold MG draws into the car park. 'Bugger.' And Rita turns her back to the vehicle, not wanting to acknowledge it.

'It is a bugger,' Graham responds, and Rita stares at row upon row of orange porous brick, tiny red spiders, tiny black ants. 'Tracie's coming round in a minute. I was going to make a meal. Dinner for two. Dad's not invited.'

'Can you get him? Let me talk to him.'

'I'll try.'

Rita hears Graham put the receiver on the hall table, she hears his shoes clop away down the hall, and she fingers the brooch on her dress bodice, the swirl of silver mirroring her churning insides.

'Rita! Darling! What you up to? Molesting the masonry!' Stevie Richmond pinches Rita's backside and she whips round, the phone still pressed to her ear. 'Pardon me,' Stevie says. 'For my importunance.'

'No matter,' says Rita. There is a vacuum at the other end of the line. 'Guests come first.' She opens her handbag and, partly relieved, partly not, flips the mobile inside. 'I'll try again later.'

'Don't think your bag goes with the rest of the ensemble, Rita,' Stevie then observes. 'Much too mocha.'

'My work bag,' Rita explains, and she smiles. She cannot help but smile. Stevie Richmond is a clown. He wears a purple lurex suit, and the suit jacket is unbuttoned to reveal a tight-fitting T-shirt. The shirt's V-neck is low and Rita can see Stevie's springy grey chest hairs, and the flick of a tattooed tail, a mermaid diving down to his flabby pectorals. 'My,' she says. 'You're—'

'Sexy,' says Stevie. 'I know, and so, woman, are you.' He looks Rita up and down, and then he offers his arm. 'Time to razzle dazzle. *N'est-ce pas?* '

So, did you get through?

I don't want to talk about it.

It might help.
Might not.
I love you.
Please.

'Nice brooch, by the way,' Celia says.

Mrs Sylvie Frink, prominent WOSB member, wife of Leslie Frink, head of the Shantung Wedding Group, forks a prawn and drops it into her mouth. She chews. 'So, has my Leslie phoned you?'

'About what?' Rita watches Sylvie search through her salad for another interesting bite.

'Sam Randel, our chief buyer, he needs someone to mind his flat.' Sylvie uncovers a grape. 'A marvellous penthouse, minimalist decor, off-white, hardly any furniture. Hasn't Leslie told you?' The fat black grape sits on Sylvie's tongue now. She flicks it forwards, catching it between her bucked front teeth.

'Yes, he's mentioned it,' Rita replies.

'So—' Sylvie chomps the grape. 'You're taking it on?'

'Can't say.'

'Why ever not?'

'My client list is confidential.'

'Oh, Rita.' Sylvie swallows. 'Rita. Rita.' She gulps. 'Serious. Serious.' She tuts. 'You're just like Leslie. Secrets. Secrets.' She tuts again. 'When's your eldest's wedding? Now you must be able to tell me that?'

'I can't.'

'Oh, come on!'

Rita swigs her wine. She can see Celia standing behind Sylvie, talking to Mr Arnold, newly arrived. 'It's nothing to do with me,' Rita says. 'Graham's unsure. He doesn't want to make a mistake.'

'But Tracie's lovely. I know her mother. They have the same black hair, very thick, there's some Italian in the family. She'd suit our new Heavenly Empress. She's more than a C cup isn't she? A floor-length dress with a daisy-covered bodice which hugs the breasts. You need to be big to carry it off. She'd get a discount. The groom too. Of course.'

'I'll let him know,' Rita replies.

Mr Arnold sips his mineral water.

'You don't drink?' asks Rita.

'I leave that to my fish and my ex-wife.' Mr Arnold puts down his glass and cuts a slither of Jarlsberg. 'I've a very loose tongue when I'm drunk.'

'Can be dangerous.'

'Yes.' Mr Arnold places the slither on a star-shaped cracker. 'Our meeting this morning was excellent, by the way.' He returns the cheese knife to its board. 'I feel very reassured.'

'Thank you.'

Mr Arnold holds his cracker to his mouth. 'And I can expect your report tomorrow?' he asks.

'Definitely.'

'Even though this is a busy time?' Mr Arnold bites into his cracker, cleanly, evenly, shedding no crumbs.

'Definitely,' Rita reasserts. 'I'm used to working under pressure.' She spots Philippa come towards them, pursued by Cornelius Abbot. The girl is smiling, flushed, rose-tinted.

'Experience,' says Mr Arnold. 'You can't beat it.'

'Did I see you with Celia Taylor?' Rita asks.

We must talk.

Rita sits on the lime-green sofa. Stevie Richmond perches awkwardly on the arm beside her. She's feeling addled. He puffs on a plump cigar. 'Isn't that sweet?' he says to her, using the cigar as a pointer.

'Those two?' she asks, watching Derek, her clumsiest sitter, with his fiancée, their plates piled with cold meats, salad stuff, bread. Derek tickles his fiancée's face with a frilly lettuce leaf.

'Cute,' says Stevie.

'No.' Rita is sure. 'An accident waiting to happen.'

'Aren't we all?' says Stevie, stubbing his cigar. 'Now, give us that.' He takes Rita's wine-glass, begins to clink it against his rings, the four gold sovereigns on the four fat fingers of his left hand. 'Listen everybody!' he shouts.

'Stevie!' Rita tugs at his lurex jacket, but he's off the sofa, pulling her up, standing her next to him.

'It's time we paid homage to our hostess,' he tells the party. Loudly. 'The gorgeous Rita Swales.'

Faces turn, conversations falter. 'Hear, hear,' someone bellows. And Dolly Parton warbles on about lost love. She wails a lonesome wail, and then, when the note dies, Stevie begins.

'A speech is in order,' he says. 'Because I adore this woman. She's tremendous. She's a big glittery Christmas ornament. OTT. She's very very special. Mae West times three. She's *je ne sais quoi* and I love her to bits. The world needs women like Rita. The business-world needs women like Rita. It needs some glamour.'

Rita pats her hair. A wolf whistles, and another yowls, 'Get her picture!' A camera flashes, flashes again.

'Enough!' orders Stevie. 'Or I'll forget my place. Yes, Rita's fleshy, and she can be mouthy.'

'Not as mouthy as you.'

'Enough!' Stevie puts his arm round Rita. 'This lady—' He has a lighter touch than Bill, not as affecting. 'Well, she does have her opinions, and she won't be stood on the mantelpiece. She's ambitious, a doer and a goer and a getter, and she puts the wind up the grey-suits. They gave her business two years but she's surprised them. I always knew she would. I think we all knew she would. Because she's a woman with a body and a mind to match. She has flair. She has guts. She has true true colour. She's shinier than most. And I know why. Because I'm the same. I'm that yellow splash-patch on the bum of your jeans, the shimmering sequins on your *Come Dancing* frock. I'm real rich reds and the perkiest pinks. I'm silvery blues. I need to be. No drab Draylon or hateful hessian. Come to Crazy Covers and you will see. Voluptuous velvets and sexy silks. I'm Mr Fabric Fantastic. With my plush plush piles and linga-longa leathers. Tormenting tassels—'

'Off,' someone shouts. 'Get him off!'

You've been ignoring me.

I've done nothing but trip over you.

You've done nothing but flirt, and not with me.

It's a party. I have to spread myself. It's what you do at parties.

That and worry about your husband. Will he turn up? Won't he?

Please.

Sorry. I'm sorry. Let's not argue.

You started it.

No, we both started it.

Please.

Remember?

'Stupendous brooch!' says Mrs Sylvie Frink.

The fruit bowl is the fullest thing on the table. Every other container, every other platter, is emptying fast. But the bowl is still flush with apples and cherries and bananas, with kumquats, kiwis and pears. Rita looks at the bananas and, as she wonders whether she fancies one and whether it would be wise to unpeel one in this company, with this crowd, she overhears Philippa talking to Bill.

‘You must be bitter,’ says Philippa.

‘No, it was all right in the beginning. Alice loved me then. I couldn’t wish that away.’

‘But after all that time,’ says Philippa.

‘Well, time’s the culprit really. It muddies things.’

Philippa pushes her tortoiseshell bangle up her arm. ‘Does it?’

‘Yes. Well, Alice said her feelings got ‘murkier’ as the years passed.’

Philippa pushes her bangle down her arm. She seems uncomfortable. ‘Still, that was no reason for her to do what she did.’

‘She found it hard to compromise.’ Bill glances about. He seems uncomfortable too. ‘But that’s why I went with her in the first place.’ His eyes meet Rita’s. She quickly looks away, fusses with the fruit. ‘She was a strong woman.’

‘Like Mrs Swales? Mrs Swales is a strong woman.’

‘Yes, like your boss. Here, listen—’

Rita bites into a cherry. She watches Bill lean towards Philippa.

‘Listen—’ Bill says again. He isn’t whispering. ‘Can I tell you a secret? I’m in love with another woman now. She’s strong, she’s gorgeous, but she burns hot and cold, and it’s beginning to get to me. You see, I’m flesh and blood—’

‘I don’t know if I’ll ever get married,’ says Philippa. ‘I don’t have much luck with men. I can’t hold their interest. They’re keen at the start, but then—’

‘And she doesn’t seem to understand that.’ Bill sighs. ‘I’m flesh and blood. I can’t wait for ever.’

Josie enters the agency, still wearing shorts, her Take Five Video Store cap pushed down on her head, its peak shadowing her eyes. But she seems happy. She nods at Rita and then sidles up to Philippa and Bill.

‘Hello,’ says Philippa. ‘Are you all right now?’

‘Never been better.’ Josie looks from Philippa to her boss. She smiles. ‘This man sorted it for me,’ she says. ‘Didn’t you, Mr Henley?’

‘I did.’ Bill tugs the peak of Josie’s cap.

Josie laughs. ‘Hey!’ And she nips Bill’s backside.

‘Hey!’ Bill grabs Josie’s pony-tail and threatens to yank it. ‘Remember who pays your wages!’

Philippa stares at her hands, her feet. ‘Well, that’s good. I’m glad it’s sorted,’ she says, colouring-up and turning away. ‘Oh, Mrs Swales!’ she then exclaims, finding herself face to face with Rita. ‘Isn’t that good?’

‘Yes,’ Rita replies. She picks out another cherry. ‘It is.’

‘He’s very fit,’ says Celia. She dabs a tissue about her lips.

‘Who? The photographer?’ asks Rita.

‘No, he smells like drains.’ Celia examines the tissue and drops it on the agency floor.

‘Who then?’ asks Rita. ‘Him over there?’ She points to Mr Arnold who sits alone on the sofa, a male model of neatness and formality, a sticky-out thumb of reserve.

‘Oh no, definitely not! I’ve had him.’

‘Never!’

‘Yep. Nice body but ex-obsessed.’ Celia then indicates her prey. ‘That’s who I mean. He’s scrumptious.’

‘Oh.’ Rita glances over at Bill, still making-a-show, larking with Josie. ‘Is he?’

‘You mean you haven’t noticed? You *are* slipping, girl!’

‘Let me guess,’ says Mrs Sylvie Frink. ‘Hoffmans? A Hoffmans’ piece?’

Rita stands in the car park, staring at Mr Fruity Man’s van, holding her mobile to her ear. She’s on the line to home, and nobody's answering. Not even Graham. The line rings and rings, and Rita shifts from foot to foot.

Mr Fruity Man's van is decorated with bananas. Some of the bananas are unpeeled and fluorescent yellow, some half-peeled, some nakedly cream. All are participating in an aerobatic display. A loop-the-loop. A twirling somersault. A daring arrowheaded formation of twenty-one bananas shooting across the van's bonnet.

Rita shakes her head. She's started seeing faces on the 'nanas, gung-ho have-a-go faces, and her back nips, and her legs ache. She's really had enough.

The number of years she's put into pleasing him, doing things for him, and now, when she wants something back, Collis won't give.

Rita returns the mobile to her bag, and she sighs. He could be on his way, proving her wrong, of course. But she doubts this. More likely he's having one of his crying fits. Collis is blubbing, and Graham's having to deal with it. Rita sighs again. She feels sorry for her son.

Rita drops a dirtied serviette into her makeshift bin, the carton from Barry's Bangers and Party Playthings. She turns on the tap, swills cake crumbs off a plate. She puts the plate on the drainer.

What's this?

Just tidying.

Why?

I need to think.

Do you know what I think about? That time in the stock-room. I think about it a lot.

You do?

Yes.

It was a quickie.

But it was good, wasn't it?

It was a good quickie.

Kiss me, Rita. We're suited in every way.
What?
Kiss me. Now. No one will see. Please.
Your admirers might see.

Derek's fiancée cleans her spectacles with the scalloped hem of her halter top. 'Don't get me wrong, Mrs Swales,' she says. 'I think it's brilliant Derek has this job. He's passionate about it, but honestly I can't see the attraction and I don't know what we're going to do when we're married. I mean he lives for weeks in other people's homes.'

'That's something you'll have to talk to Derek about,' Rita replies.

'You see,' says Derek's fiancée. She holds her spectacles up to her face, examining the lenses. 'I believe marriage is about staying put and settling down. It's going to be a real test for us. And Derek's going to feel awfully dissatisfied coming back to our modest – and with his wage (no offence) it will be modest – marital home after spending all that time in some businessman's mansion.'

'It's you, not the house, he'll be coming back to.' Rita looks about for a get-out. She sees Molly Thorn, standing by the lime two-seater sofa, with an apple in her hand. Rita smiles and waves. 'It'll be no different from being married to someone working the oil rigs.'

'I can't see my Derek on an oil rig,' says his fiancée.

'It's a shame about your husband. He should be here to help you celebrate,' says Molly, who works for Cranley Tourist Information. 'Because you've done really well. Most businesses fold in their first year.'

'Mmm,' Rita replies, half-looking at Molly, half-looking through the agency window at the traffic passing by and hoping Collis isn't about to arrive. Because she's told Molly he's sick. Because she's telling everyone he's sick now. Because she's fed-up skirting, avoiding those ever-so polite enquiries about him.

'I mean, we're always updating our B&B lists. One or two close every month, especially those right in the city.' Molly bites into her apple.

'But they're hardly on to a winner there, are they?' Rita comments. A bus stops opposite. 'Cranley's somewhere you want to escape from, not visit.' Rita glimpses the ad pasted between the top and lower decks. A smiling bride in a flouncy princess gown – *Make your day a Shantung Gown day.*

'Your husband, Mrs Swales?' the photographer asks, tucking a lock of greasy hair behind his ear. 'Has he turned up? Only I've got to go soon.'

'No,' Rita says. 'He hasn't.'

'Only Jenny 90 wanted a photo of the two of you together.'

'He isn't here. He won't ever be here. He's sick.'

'Oh.' The photographer fiddles with his camera strap.

'Will I do instead?' Stevie Richmond appears beside Rita. 'I'm far more handsome than her husband.' He smiles at the photographer. 'And I've a caption too – *The King and Queen of Flash and Frolics.* How about that?'

Bill passes, pursued by Josie, by Celia. 'Who's the Queen?' he calls.

'Oooh, *très* witty!' Stevie replies, putting his face next to Rita's, grinning cheesily. 'Ready?'

'No,' says the photographer. 'It's not what I'm after.'

'What's the problem?' Stevie asks.

'You've got two legs,' Rita says. She smells Stevie's aftershave. It is heady and sickly like Parma Violets. 'That's the problem.'

'Good evening, Mrs Swales,' greets John Whittaker,

Rita's longest-serving sitter. He wears a summer suit but carries an umbrella.

'John,' Rita says. 'You're surely not expecting rain?'

'When it's as close as this, Mrs Swales.' John Whittaker fixes her with his steady gaze. 'I expect the Heavens to open.'

Rita stares at herself in the toilet mirror. Not bad, considering. The wine has brought a pinkish glow to her face, and it suits her. She retouches her lipstick, fluffs her hair, and smoothes her frock. She unlocks the toilet door.

And a tango plays.

'Thought it might be you.' Bill blocks her way.

'Bill, please,' Rita says. 'Let me by.'

'Can't.'

'Or won't?' Rita considers ducking under Bill's outstretched arms, his big hands clutching the doorframe.

'Can't,' Bill confesses, looking at her, his deep-set eyes pinning her. 'I just can't.'

'We've been over this.' Rita sighs. 'This isn't the time or the place.'

'I know you like me,' he replies.

'There's lots of women who like you,' she says. 'Unattached women. They're chasing after you.'

'Uninteresting women.'

'Unattached women,' Rita reasserts.

Bill rocks on his feet. He seems very drunk. 'I wish there were no complications. I wish we'd met years ago.'

'You can't turn the clock back.' Rita is firm. 'Besides, we probably wouldn't have had that much in common. I wasn't a business woman. I lived in Crossforth. Collis was right for me then.'

'Then?' Bill moves closer.

'Stop.' Rita puts out a hand.

'I can give you so much,' he whispers. 'I'm not afraid of you, Rita. I want to support you. I wouldn't make you do the dishes. I want you to be Business Woman of the Year. I believe in you.'

'You've got cheese on your chin,' says Rita.

'Then flick it off.'

The tango slides round Rita's guests, slithers up and shimmies down them, the hot sexy sound causing even the tightest (not Mr Arnold, he's gone home) to loosen and laugh louder, to quaff and scoff more; causing most to sway and wiggle their hips, to make extravagant claims for their businesses and hand-shake dubious deals, to declare affection, swear affiliation, swap five year plans, star-signs, and successful scams.

Kiss me, Rita.

'How's your brother?' Rita asks Stevie.

'The same, still popping the pills, still afraid to go outdoors.' A dribble of red runs from the corner of Stevie's mouth. He wipes it away with the back of his besovereigned hand. 'And your sick man?' he asks. 'How's he?'

'Worse.' Rita sighs, spying Celia moving in on Bill, tapping his shoulder. 'We just don't have any fun. I can't remember the last time we had any fun. It's a constant battle.'

'Don't give up on him though,' says Stevie.

'Why ever not?'

Celia has a carnation clamped between her teeth. She waves her arms in the air, then wraps them round Bill's middle. She encourages him to dance.

'Because I gave up on my Malcolm once, and I didn't know if I was coming or going, hithering or thithering.'

Celia throws her head back, rucks up her skirt to show off her thighs.

'Save me,' Bill mouths to Rita.

'Can't,' she returns.

'He brings me down to earth,' continues Stevie, as Rita watches Josie – her baseball cap pulled rakishly over one eye – pushing between Celia and Bill.

'Sorry?' Rita says to Stevie. 'I missed that.'

'My brother's a leveller,' Stevie shouts, as Bill refuses his assistant, turns his back on both her and Celia. 'Without him and his problems, I'd go *VAMOOSE* !' Stevie jabs the air with his thumb. 'Up my own *derrière*.'

Bill appears beside Rita. 'What's this?' he asks.

'Mrs Swales—' Doreen stands before Rita. Her cheeks are pink, her eyes watery, hyphenated by the graze on her nose which has become a florid dash of purple now. 'The Gallaghers have a guinea pig. I wasn't told about a guinea pig. It's not in the contract, and I don't know his likes or dislikes. I'm frightened I'll kill him. I don't know anything about guinea pigs.'

'Treat him like a rabbit,' Rita snaps. 'You've looked after rabbits.'

'Yes, but—'

'And I'll charge them for it, don't you worry.'

'What's this?' Bill asks, appearing beside her.

'So, your husband couldn't come?'

'No,' Rita confirms. 'Unfortunately not. He's not feeling very well.'

'What a shame,' says Mrs Janet Armouth, a member of Greenacres W.I. and one of Rita's regular clients. 'Nothing serious, I hope? Nothing to do with his—' Mrs Janet Armouth nods at Rita's legs.

'His injuries?' Rita obliges.

'When I think what that poor man must've gone through,' Mrs Janet Armouth reflects. 'Chopped off in his prime.'

'What's this?' asks Bill, appearing beside them.

Rita sighs. 'Collis,' she explains. 'Mrs Armouth was just sympathising.'

'Yes,' Bill offers. 'It's not been easy for Mr Swales. It's not been easy for Mrs Swales either.'

'But what I've always wondered, and tell me if I'm being nosy here,' Mrs Janet Armouth persists. 'What I've always wondered is how the compensation was calculated? You see, my nephew's just lost his finger in a flying accident.'

'Mrs Armouth, this is a party,' Bill protects. 'I'm sure Mrs Swales doesn't want to—'

'It's okay.' Rita moves from Bill. She stares at Mrs Armouth. 'My husband got hurt at work,' she says. 'His accident was an industrial accident.'

'I'm aware of that,' Mrs Armouth replies. 'But there must be a chart which tells the judges whether a pinkie is worth more than an ear-lobe and by how much. Nuts-and-bolts stuff which'll be the same for injuries sustained,' Mrs Janet Armouth smiles, 'wherever.'

'There's different sums for different body parts,' Rita acquiesces.

'I thought so.' Mrs Janet Armouth smiles some more. She leans against the buffet table. 'And what else? Do they price up the intangibles, like emotional distress? My nephew's wetting his bed, poor soul.'

'Yes, that and—'

'And?' presses Mrs Janet Armouth.

'Family circumstances, prognosis.'

'Indeed,' says Mrs Janet Armouth.

'Basically.' Rita folds her arms. 'The court decided my husband was on the scrap heap. He had no future. His future had been taken from him. That's why he was awarded what many people, I know, regard as an exorbitant amount.'

'Oh, exorbitant. Is that what people say? How terrible.' Mrs Janet Armouth takes a kiwi from the fruit bowl. She strokes it as she would a little pet. 'Terrible.'

Rita. Surrounded. By guests, by noise, by the hot red tips of cigarettes, by business cards and clinking glasses, hands gesticulating, polished and varnished nails, a wart on a knuckle, a diamond solitaire, a scar running ragged round a wrist.

Rita. Agreeing. Responding. Disagreeing. Smiling. Laughing. Smacking her lips. Tasting her lipstick. Still there. Pushing a finger down her cleavage, feeling the moistness. Patting her frock bodice. Feeling the brooch. Aware of him. There.

'I love you, friend,' Celia tells Rita.

'I should phone Collis,' Rita replies.

'Why? He made the choice. He didn't want to come.'

'He's in a state.'

'He's always in a state. The selfish tears of a weak man—'

'What?'

'—drown many a good woman,' Celia says. Then. 'Does that sound right?'

'Christ knows. Who told you that?'

'A little fatty called Cornelius. Him over there. Look. He cried many selfish tears when I said no to dinner at Wilson's, and now he's trying it on with Philippa.'

Cornelius Abbot and Philippa stand by the filing-cabinet. Cornelius Abbot cups a wine-glass in his hands. He says something to Philippa which makes her smile, her face fill with pleasure.

'Yuk.' Celia grimaces.

'You turned down Wilson's?' Rita then asks.

'Had to. There's only one man for me now.'

'And he's not a little fatty?'

'Right. He's called Bill Henley, and I just want to check something here.' Celia looks at Rita. 'He's not after you, is he? Only he's round you an awful lot.'

'So, you can stay in your house?' Rita says to Josie.

The video-store assistant nods. She pulls her ponytail over her shoulder, examines the hair for split ends, and asks, 'What is it between you and my boss?'

'What do you mean, exactly?' Rita tries not to sound defensive.

'You know.' Josie tugs at a strand, pulls it out.

'No, I don't.'

'Mrs Swales, I realise I don't count for much, what I think and feel.' Josie winds the strand tightly round her little finger, causing the skin at its tip to turn dark purple, the angry colour masking the mini-tattoo *S 4 J*.

'Josie, you know that isn't true,' Rita tells her. 'I gave you flowers at dinner-time, I listened to you, I invited you—'

Josie holds up her finger. 'Some people have all the luck,' she then says. 'They have everything. A nice house, a career, a man who lets them do what they want, and still they think the grass'll be greener, still they're not satisfied. I don't understand it.'

'You'd better unwind that.' Rita is cool. 'Before you lose your nail.'

Rita heads for the sofa. She needs to sit. But Joanna and Nolene are already there, snuggled together. Nolene plucking fern from Joanna's hair. Joanna laughing, huskily.

'Oh, what a lovely brooch!' exclaims Miss Sheila Harcourt, another one of Rita's sitters. And the Honourable Sherwin Oxford (Cranley's Mayor), Mrs Susie Timmins (another regular client), and Mr Arthur Brace (the agency's stationery supplier) concur.

'Thank you,' says Rita.

'From an admirer?' enquires Mr Arthur Brace, a wimpy fellow with a bulbous chin like the underside of a spoon, who once pursued her ardently himself. 'I'd do anything for you. Please allow me to,' he begged, and Rita felt like laughing, telling him where to go, except she had to turn him down politely, let him down lightly, not wishing to upset him and endanger her 'fifty for the price of thirty' deal on resealable manilas.

'Please.' Rita smiles. 'I'm much too old for admirers.'

'You're never too old,' says the Honourable Sherwin Oxford. He takes a hanky from his pocket and starts to polish his chain of office.

'What's this?' Bill asks, suddenly appearing behind Rita, his words upon her neck, the button mole she has at the top of her spine.

'Just chit chat.' Rita is cold.

'Oh.' Bill hesitates. Then. 'Look. There's something I need to say. There's something I have to say.'

'Not now, Mr Henley.' Rita steps back on his loafers, skewering him with her heels. He takes in a breath.

'Well?' enquires Mr Arthur Brace. 'What? What do you have to say?'

'Videos,' blurts Bill. 'We cater for all tastes, from young to old, from art-house to gore-house. That's Take Five Video Store. Take Five Video Store, thousands of videos, spoilt for choice!'

'Hehehe,' giggles Mrs Susie Timmins.

Sorry.

'Gangway,' someone shouts.

'Puke alert!'

'Honestly!'

'How awful.'

Nolene moves speedily, her body crouched forwards,

heading for the toilet, a serviette clamped over her mouth.

'Oh dear.' Joanna Holland sighs. 'I could see that coming.'

'No doubt.' Rita slides on to the sofa, into the spot Nolene has vacated. She puts a hand on her head, trying to still the hyperactivity inside. 'Nolene has a tendency to vomit at our events.'

'She's nice, though, isn't she?' Joanna says, twiddling one of her diamanté droplets. 'Very attractive.'

Rita's eyebrows raise, quizzically, askance.

'But, I must confess,' continues Joanna. 'I'm finding it difficult, starting-over. I don't know if I really want to. I left my partner a while back, we'd been together for ten years, we were having the most terrible rows and actually I didn't fancy her any more, but I miss her. I never expected to. But we'd got comfortable together and, you know, had built a life together.'

'Her?'

'Yes.' Joanna stares at Rita. She no longer twiddles her droplet. 'They were very good about it at Vinvictor's. They had a very enlightened equal opps policy. Angela and I were given the same perks as the married and cohabiting heterosexuals who worked there. Free sheaths.'

'Free sheaths?'

'Free sheaths. We made them.'

'You could hardly use them,' says Rita.

'No, but the principle was important. Equal shares. What about your policy, Mrs Swales—'

Derek trips, showering wine over his fiancée.

'Sorry we're late.' Rita's accountant arrives with a party of five.

'How many times!' Derek's fiancée cries. 'You oaf! You fucking oaf!'

Rita watches Bill and Josie. He's saying something to her and she seems upset, her mouth is pinched, her pointy jaw tensed. She looks across at Rita, and Rita looks away.

'Ah, Mrs Swales.'

Rita's accountant approaches, thrusting out his hand for her to shake. She eases herself up from the sofa.

'A thousand apologies,' he says.

'No matter.' She clasps his thin palm. It makes her shiver; this and the sudden black cloud passing over the sun, darkening the street, her office and party; this and the thought of loose boozy tongues. Bill's, for sure. Josie's, probably. Even her own. 'There's some drink left,' she says to the accountant. 'But not much food. I'm afraid you've missed the best of it.'

'We'll manage,' he replies. Then, 'Hey!'

Josie barges past, knocking the accountant forward. Unable to save himself, he grabs Rita, his mouth meeting her neck, his tie lapping her cleavage. She pushes him off.

'Sorry,' he says. 'Whoops.' He smiles.

'You're forgiven,' Rita replies, seeing Josie belt through the door, off along the road.

She made a pass. I turned her down. Cross my heart.

It's not funny, Bill. I don't find this funny. I think you should go home.

Why?

I've worked hard for this.

I know.

I'm in control of it. I like being in control. I want to stay in control. Understand?

I'm only flesh and blood, Rita.

'Phone!'

'Somebody's mobile?'

'A phone's ringing!'

Rita leaves by the back door. She blinks as she leans against the agency's rear wall. The black cloud has shifted and the sun shines bright, heightening and burnishing every reflective surface around her: the Give Way sign by the car park's entrance, the yellow plastic grit bin, the cars. There's the glaring metallic bronze of Bill's estate and the blaring scarlet of Celia's Jeep and the whiter than white of her own four-door saloon and the vile jade of Mr Fruity Man's van. All gleaming like they've been treated with tubs of turtle wax.

'Oh, you're so funny.' The voice rises above the shenanigans, the partying-on, and gusts out the open door. 'Tell us another one,' it demands.

Rita knows the voice. Its loudness gives it away. A voice which once upon a time had to contend with the rattling humming whirr of overlocking machines.

'A blue one,' the voice pesters. 'Tell us a blue one.'

It's accompanied by the sound of heels clipping across the tiled floor of the staff quarters, and the heavier footfalls of someone, probably a man, following.

'Would you just stay still? Okay, here's a good one.'

Yes, a man, and Rita knows his voice too.

'A good blue one?' Celia asks.

Rita moves further along the wall, turning her back to the agency, the flirting, the punch line and laughter, and she looks along the rear of the shops. A strip of shade nestles close to the buildings and a tramp, fiftyish, with salt'n'pepper hair, shuffles down it. He stops by the black bins and the mounds of rubbish outside Garsten Street Delicatessen and Restaurant, and fumbles with his trouser zip. Rita wonders whether to shoo him away, tell him to scat. He takes out his penis and she decides against it, feeling much too tired to deal with a probable nutter and his organ. She will stick to her own business.

She finds her mobile and presses the numbers for home, watching the tramp's piss steaming from him, circulating mistily round his feet, obscuring his boots but not the thin, flapping material of his flannels, the raggy hem of his jacket.

All that is mine I carry with me ...

'Yes?' Graham's voice.

'Hello, darling,' Rita says.

'What happened to you? I tried to get you. Twice.'

'Clients, the party. I've tried you too.' Rita pauses, and the tramp does up his fly, hoicks his flannels by the waistband, reminding her of her father, of every man she's ever known. 'How's Dad?' she asks as the tramp digs into the rubbish, pulling out a knapsack which he swings effortfully over his shoulder.

My coat and bag are my home ...

'He's sorted. Jimmy's taken him out, is dropping him off somewhere.'

'Dropping him off? Where? Here? Is Dad coming here? Now?'

I am oppressed ...

'No, not to the party. Jimmy's meeting his mates and is dropping Dad off on the way, somewhere, Crossforth maybe.'

I am oppressed by roots ...

'What?'

'Crossforth.'

Permanence ...

'What's he playing at?'

Fixtures ...

'Who knows? Anyway, Mum, it's sorted, and Tracie's here. We're talking.'

'You want me to hang up?'

'Please.' Rita can hear soft salivary kissing noises, rustling, a giggle. 'Look, Mum.' Graham is losing it, his voice whispery. 'Must go. Have to go.'

'Okay.' Rita imagines her white-haired son pressed up against the hall wall, his black-haired fiancée pleasuring him. 'Bye,' she says, feeling happy for him, feeling suddenly scared.

But I am getting old now ...

The tramp is wandering between the parked cars. He comes to Mr Fruity Man's van, and looks across at Rita. He runs a finger along one of the bananas. He smiles, and Rita blanks him.

I cannot wait for ever.

Collis

My wife is complicated. She wasn't when we first met. Then she was as simple as anything. Not dense because she does have a brain. But you could tell what she was about, you could understand her. You could see it in the way she dressed, in the way she moved. She was a physical girl, all instincts, into living for the day, and into us.

The kids killed all that. And it took me an age to realise what was happening. I was working all hours, getting the money in, keeping the roof over our heads. I thought I was doing all right. But Rita was losing herself. She was coming apart, slipping away.

My accident *was* an accident but sometimes I think I willed it, sometimes I think I wanted her back so much it had to happen. I made that machine start up on me. And, in the beginning, when I was in hospital, not in the real world, I actually thought I'd done some good. Rita got to grips. With each visit she appeared lovelier, happier, warmer. She held me. Her seemingly straight-as-a-die, gutsy self.

I was longing to get home. I thought it'd be great. I'd

lost a leg and some fingers but really thought it would be better. Me and Rita like we used to be. Me and Rita, husband and wife, parents. One big happy family.

I was, still am, a fool.

I've missed her party. I'm sorry about that. But I wasn't about to be exhibited, talked at, sympathised over. I am a fool but I am also me. She used to love me for being me.

I'm on my own a lot now. The boys are older, usually out, and Rita has her business. I spend most days in the garden, weeding. Dr Shah says I'm depressed. I'm grieving for my leg and fingers, he says. But once upon a time everything was simple. I knew, I thought I knew, where we'd be.

I'm a mess. I have to face it.

A fool and a mess who threw his wedding photo at the wall. The glass broke, but we're still there, under the splinters, her head on my shoulder, smiling. She's wearing a top you can see her skin through. She's never been ashamed. Flaunt it. Use it. She was the easiest girl in Crossforth.

But still I couldn't believe it when she let me. She was my first, my only, and she'll always be. I've never wanted anyone else. Because we're both from there, and what we found together turned the empty into full. Rita knows that. She's not the fool. No matter how much she's changed. She'll find it difficult to turn her back on that.

Call it a Day

Rita unzips her handbag and fumbles for her purse. The taxi driver leans into the rear of the cab, watching. 'You all right?' he asks.

Rita opens her purse – 'Fine. Fine' – and removes a tenner. 'Keep the change,' she murmurs, handing it to him as she pushes herself out.

'Thanks.' The driver shoves the note in his trouser pocket and takes Rita's arm. 'This isn't the safest area to be in,' he says, helping her from the cab. 'Not for someone who's a bit—' He looks at Rita, reconsiders his words. 'Not for a lady on her own.'

Rita drops her purse in her bag. 'I'll be okay. Nothing to worry about,' she asserts. She refastens her bag and clutches it tightly against her stomach. 'I'm from here. I can handle it. Besides, I'm meeting someone.'

It was one of those stalemate Sundays, a month back. Rita wanted to go through some papers for work. Collis wanted to do something 'special' together.

'What's your problem?' Collis said. 'Why can't you take a look?'

'I don't have a problem,' Rita replied.

'Well, let's go then. Take a trip out.'

'No.' Rita patted her thick insurance file. 'I've no time, it'll take too long, I've got to get on with this.'

'Got to do this,' Collis said. 'Got to do that.'

Rita sighed. 'Okay, we'll go to the Jubilee, for food and a drink. How about that?'

'Not interested,' Collis replied.

Rita watches the taxi go. She grips her bag, feeling nauseous, knowing it has nothing to do with the drink. She begins to walk.

'I want to see it,' said Collis. 'And I want to see it with you.'

'But why?' said Rita. 'Everything changes. The building site's gone. The High's a skills centre for the unemployed. We've changed. Nothing stays the same.'

She turns into the street. Her mouth is dry and she swallows as she looks about her. The street is empty. There are no people, not even Collis. The road has been resurfaced, the pavement patched. There's a shrub in a wooden tub and there are square yellow bins, their rusted pedestals littered with crisp packets, fag packets, cans. Walls are fly-postered. The streetlamps have metal, not concrete, shafts. It is not the same, and Rita smiles and walks on. She can handle this.

'I want to see it,' said Collis. 'And I want to see it with you.'

'But why?' said Rita.

'It's important to me.'

'I'm not ready for memory lane,' she said.

‘Collis!’ she shouts.

Perhaps he hasn’t arrived yet.

‘Collis!’

He could be struggling along the tow-path by the canal, or taking a rest, huddling mournfully beneath the arch of Iron Bridge. Perhaps he’s by the twin towers, negotiating the pavement’s ruts and hollows.

‘Collis!’

Or perhaps he’s spotted her and is hiding.

He could be watching from a darkened doorway.

‘Come on!’ Rita shouts. ‘Show yourself!’

She shivers. She walks more briskly. She pulls her jacket about her, wishing she’d put a couple of miniatures in her handbag, tots of gin and whisky. She’s beginning to sober up. She passes some posters, unglossy ads for Crossforth’s Credit Union, the SlimAway Club, line-dancing at Yolanda’s, and Do-U-Need-A-Loan? She sees a photo of a mini-cab and a giant-sized arrow pointing to nowhere, to a gap between the posters, a cold strip of stone. She stares at the stone.

‘Collis!’

She reaches the Guild and Union shields set into the paving, and comes to one of the pillars marking the entrance to Cranley’s Industrial Laundry.

‘Collis!’ she bellows. ‘Collis!’

Where is he? Is he behind this pillar waiting? Just like she waited for him once, crouched by the fluted weathered stone, a factory girl nervously waiting for a schoolboy to come from the High.

Rita glances around the pillar. No. She glances round the next. Not there either. She glances at the Laundry gates. They are locked. They never used to be.

The Laundry worked around the clock, cleaning and steaming, pressing and packing, as day turned to night, night into day. Rita peers between the gate rails into the Laundry’s floodlit yard. She sees the red-bricked barn of a building and the tall tower, the funnel of fumes, projecting from its rear. Just as it was.

Except the floodlights are bigger and brighter, and the building's frontage glitters with multicoloured tiles. There's a neon sign – BB'S BARGAINS – and fluorescent banners advertising sock bundles, thong panties, hat and glove sets, novelty ties, fake fur muffs. Almost as it was.

Except there is no outhouse tacked to the building's side. There is no McGee's.

Rita stares.

Gone. Replaced by nothing but a flattened strip of land tarmacked salmon-pink, rain clouds drifting slow across the grey Crossforthian sky.

Gone, and she realises she wanted to see her window.

The streetlamps flicker on.

'Hang on a minute,' Celia said. 'Where has *he* come from?'

Rita fumbles inside her jacket. She unclips Bill's brooch and lets it drop.

'He's gorgeous.' Celia swooned. 'He's ripe.'

'Collis?'

A cat belts from the cobbled passage which bordered McGee's and now the pink tarmac. The short-cut which connected this street to the shops and houses behind. The high-walled alley which was crammed with dustbins and empty boxes, crates and polythene bags, and, occasionally, a boy and a girl, drawn hungrily together.

'Jesus! Scat!' The cat crosses Rita's feet, its tail tonguing her legs and she kicks out, missing it, seeing it scamper past the whirl of silver caught in the glow of the nearest lamp. Rita shakes her head and puts her hand to her chest. What was she thinking of?

She can't leave it here. It was wrong to ditch it. A worker from BB'S Bargains may find it and – not realising its value – give it to his daughter to play dress-up with. Or someone may tread on it and squash it flat. Or Collis may notice it, and it isn't for Collis to see, even here, on the ground, discarded. She'll have to retrieve it and return it to Bill, because Bill will ask her about it, maybe even ask her to wear it again, ever persistent, stupid, hopeful. That'll be the best move. Return the gift, she decides; get rid of it properly, make her intentions plain.

Rita scoops up the brooch and slips it into her handbag, seeing Bill's big fingers picking it from a tray in the jeweller's, holding it before his piggy eyes. Yes, that's the one I want.

The one I want.

His tie was knotted loose and pulled away from the collar of a white crease-resistant shirt. The top button of the shirt was undone and there, displayed, was his thick body hair, curling from his chest to lace his beefy neck. He was smiling wide. 'Hey!' he called. 'Hey!'

'Collis?'

Rita can hear the slow padding of his crutches, his foot pressing on the alley cobbles, lifting up again, swinging into the next step, and she loops her handbag over her shoulder, wondering what to do.

Should she face him? Bawl him out like she intended to, letting him know he can't keep messing her about, he must sort himself out, she is fed up and wants. What? She is here on impulse, and on impulse decides she should scarper quick, because she has not thought this through.

'Hey!'

Too late.

'Hey! Rita!' Collis shouts. 'What's this?'

Rita glances at the alley, glimpsing only grey stone, black cobbles, no husband. 'What's what?' she asks, as a whine suddenly fills the air, needy and piercing. The cat calling out, crying for some company. Graham, Jimmy, Donny, Ben. They all sounded like that as babies, wanting their milk, sleep, her attention. Collis too, after his accident, he sounded like that for a time. A dreadful noise which drove her round the bend.

'What you doing here?' Collis shouts, as the whining comes again, from over the road, and Rita follows it, not really knowing why, hurrying away from him, to the High. 'What's going on?'

Collis began to get pains a few months after his accident. He described them to Rita. The pains were like cramps, excruciating, seizing and knotting his muscles. They distressed him because they affected the parts that'd gone, his missing leg, his fingers. He'd clutch at the pains and he'd be clutching air, nothingness. Rita called him mad. The consultant called him normal.

'Do not worry,' he said. 'Your mind is confused. Trauma has disorientated it. Even though it has registered your accident, it still thinks of you as two-legged, eight-fingered. As a consequence it is sending messages of pain beyond your points of amputation. It's not unusual. The sensations you're experiencing are in the here and now, but essentially they're not real. They're phantom, ghostly visitations, connected to the past. They will either vanish with time or, if the mind decides it feels safer with them, they'll stay.'

The High's huge iron gate has been freshly painted, in grey, and a heavy new chain secures it. Rita grabs the gate railings and they bite cold into her cheeks as she pushes her face up close. She stares fixedly into the school yard.

The cat is sitting by the tree. It has quietened. So has Collis.

He no longer shouts to her but Rita can feel him, sense his presence still. He's at the alley mouth, looking across. She can feel his eyes on her back, looking her up, down.

A drop of wet falls on her hand, and she shudders.

It's the same tree, the one she used to watch him leaning against, pressing his head, his shoulders, his buttocks against. He'd bend one long leg, flatten the sole of his shoe against the chipped and scored bark, and he'd look slowly, appraisingly about. A boy in a purple blazer, grey trousers, white shirt opened at the neck.

'And if they stay?' asked Rita. 'How's he supposed to live with them?'

'He'll find a way.'

More drops fall, heavily on the back of her hands. She tries to brush them off. Her wedding band and eternity ring catch against a railing.

Sometimes the schoolboy would glance at the factories and then Rita imagined he could see her through the small-paned window. He affected Rita. His eyes meeting her eyes. She felt, she knew, he was special.

The drops come faster, splattering on Rita's head, her shoulders, round her feet. She glances up, water skitters madly on her brow, and she lets go of the railings, raises her hands to her blow-wave. The curls are flattening. She has no umbrella.

'Hair's a bit of a mess, Rita,' Ernest observed.

And the sky breaks.

'Rita!' The voice struggles through the rushing rain.

Collis? Rita can barely hear it. Is it him again?

'It's chucking it! Come on!'

'You what?' Rita turns.

He is at the alley's mouth, standing where the cobbles finish and the street starts. He's framed by alley walls and filthy sky. He looks drenched, and Rita smiles. He's in his party clothes, and rain slaps against him, weighting and dragging the shape from his lovely suit and tie. Serves him right. He looks a sight. Then she realises, she must too.

'It's the cream dress, a daywear dress, knee-length, but a gorgeous one.'

The hem of her silky frock is clinging to her calves.

'Good choice,' Celia told Rita.

The downpour is unceasing.

'It shows off your assets.'

It beats on Rita, and the neckline of her dress catches the fall, contains it, her breasts pear-white in a brimming bowl.

'Now look at you,' scoffed Ernest.

Rita yanks her jacket over her head.

'Rita,' Collis shouts. 'Come here. This way.'

Rita fumbles to open her bag, to find her mobile, to phone for a taxi.

'Come on,' Collis shouts. 'Follow me.' He turns his back to her and slowly, carefully, moves up the alley.

Rita feels her father's video. She feels the fan with the helicopter-shaped blades, Bill's brooch, her body spray, the cotton-wool balls. She can't locate the mobile, and the bag's velvety insides are sucking up the wet, becoming soggy. A sour smell pervades the air. The Crossforthian Stretch fouling like it did, like it always will. It gets up her nose, it always did, and she coughs. Water streams from her. She zips the bag, looking at the alley, and at Collis there, pushing up it, his shoulders, his entire body, hunched tight over his crutches, struggling against the driving rain. Her pitiful husband, battling.

'My name is Rita,' she said as she kissed him.

'Collis,' he replied.

'Collis,' she said. 'Nice.'

'Wait up!' she suddenly shouts, finding herself zigzagging past puddles, across the road – her jacket pulling from her head, exposing her hair – the rain crashing down on her, running as fast as she can, as fast as fear will allow. 'Wait for me!' Her growing fear of slipping, tripping, falling to the ground, of it all washing away from her, of it all rushing out to get her, everything he protected her from.

Agnes. Ernest. The school kids. The factory. The being nothing. The dirt. The shit. No choice. No standing tall.

He was her shelter.

She was his.

Rita launches into the alley. The cobbles beneath her feet are oily, greased with wet, and her heels can't handle them. She's skating. She has jelly legs. 'Collis!' she shouts. 'Hey!'

'Rita?' Collis stops. He manoeuvres round, using one crutch as a pivot, and he looks at Rita, and she looks at him.

Hey.

He appears blurred, his outline made fuzzy by the

poor alley lighting, the fast-flowing rain. He appears too far away.

She flounders, trying to narrow the gap between them. 'This is impossible,' she calls.

Hey.

'Take it slow,' Collis advises. 'Move near the wall. It's drier there.'

Rita edges sideyways. She stretches out, puts a hand flat against the grey clammy stone.

'That's right, use it to keep you up.'

Rita reaches her husband. She is able to see him clearly now: his face glistening as if with sweat, his thick black hair matted, ropy strands drawing diagonal lines across his brow. He looks shattered. He looks embarrassed. His eyes skirt and pass over her. 'Only a little further,' he says, glancing at the sky, down at his foot, the rubber stoppers on his crutches.

Once upon a time I met a boy and he did it for me, and it seemed right, everything seemed right.

'I do know, Collis,' Rita snaps. She lets go of the wall and straightens herself, pulls herself up tall. She untwists her handbag strap, straightens it over her shoulder. She works the scooped neck of her dress and rids it of water. She reaches for her jacket pockets. 'I have been here before.' But she can't find her pockets. Her jacket is open wide, the unbuttoned fronts flattened back, plastered to her sides. 'I can't believe this,' she says then, tugging at the fronts. 'It's supposed to be summer, boiling hot, desert time.'

Collis leans forward. 'Here,' he says.

Rita holds her breath as he touches her. She feels his good hand teasing, fiddling with her jacket. She feels his fingers peeling it free from her dress. She feels his knuckles brushing her dress, and she recalls Bill slyly touching her in the car park, unhooking her keys. Hello Gorgeous. Morning Decrepit. 'Well,' she says.

The rain is less manic.

Her husband's head is bowed. His hand is still and weighty on her waist. He seems unable to move it. 'It's not how I remember it,' he says then. 'Where we went, the first time. It's grubbier, darker. There's no colour.'

She is tentative. 'Colour?'

The rain has an easier rhythm.

'I remember red.'

It is almost soothing.

'What kind of red?'

'Fiery. Flames.' He fans his fingers on to the mound of her stomach. 'What do you remember, Rita?'

Once upon a time everything was simple.

'You were keen.' A droplet of wet glides off her fringe, down her nose, and she sniffs. 'You were very keen,' she says.

Collis raises his head.

Oh.

And he stares at her, his dark eyes staring straight into her, causing her stomach to flip beneath his fingers, everything inside her to flip, despite herself.

'Rita,' he says.

Yes?

Collis's fingers press hard against her. She senses he is tilting, off balance, one crutch slipping from under his armpit. He pulls away, continuing to stare at her, his eyes never shifting from her. He rights himself, and touches her again, this time gently, stroking her with his thumb, a knuckle ridge, his bad hand now, circling her stomach, round.

'I'm a fuck-up,' he says.

Yes.

Circling.

'And I'm jealous,' he says.

Yes.

Tracing round.

‘I’m a mess,’ he says. He slides his bad hand down. ‘Rita.’

‘Yes?’

‘I don’t know a thing about housesitting,’ he says. ‘I’m sorry.’

Yes.

‘But you can train me up. I’ll come in the mornings. I’ll open the post, answer the phone.’

I’ve got my girls.

‘Philippa.’ Rita moves against his hand. ‘Nolene.’

‘Sorry,’ he says. ‘You’ve got your girls.’

‘Shush.’ Rita moves against his hand. ‘No more sorries.’ She is melting. ‘Sorry this, sorry that.’

Apologies are not what I’m about. Never were.

‘Rita.’

Yes.

Never will be.

‘You’re one helluva woman,’ he says.

Yes.

Forty-eight years old, and going through the Change, but not diminished. Sometimes she feels her skin can hardly contain her. Her energy, her ideas, her ambition.

‘I’ll make it up to you, Rita,’ he promises. His little white teeth show when he smiles. His gums pale and prominent. His lips too lovely for a man.

‘My name is Rita,’ she says.

A slinky Cupid’s bow.

‘Swales,’ Collis says.

Full-bottomed, pulsing ripe.

‘Yes,’ she says. I know. I’m forty-eight years old, full-bottomed, going through the Change, and pulsing ripe. ‘I’m Mrs Rita Swales,’ she says, and she feels fit to burst.